THE DOUBLE MAN

ALSO BY EANDO BINDER

Adam Link, Robot
The Double Man
The Eando Binder MEGAPACK®
Enslaved Brains
The Forgotten Colony
The Impossible World
The Mind from Outer Space

THE SAUCER SERIES

Menace of the Saucers
Night of the Saucers

THE DOUBLE MAN

EANDO BINDER

WILDSIDE PRESS

To Wade Wellman and our report.

CHAPTER 1

The aluminum coffin, glinting brightly in the unobscured sunlight, swung high to an apogee of 33,261 miles above earth. Then it plunged sickeningly, at ever increasing speed, to a perigee of 486 miles, whiplashing around earth to once again make the climb to its high point. Every 10 hours and 16 minutes the silent spacecraft fulfilled its eternal cycle, unvarying by a hair.

Inside, on a g-couch, lay a spacesuited figure, rigid in frozen death, his sightless eyes seeing nothing of the grand wheeling of the stars with each circling orbit. The breath of life had long since left Dr. Wayne Durk, astronaut. His gloved right hand still gripped the toggle for manual control—the toggle that he had frantically flipped again and again without response from the retro-rockets. And with the automatic system already knocked out by the meteoroid, that had been the last hope of returning to earth.

The meteoroid. It had come smashing through the cylindrical spacecraft, a rare one of baseball size, ripping apart vital wires and wrecking chains of switches and relays. Air had rushed out of the vent and only quick sealing of his spacesuit had kept Durk alive—for a slower death.

The oxygen-feed system from the craft had also phased out and he had to close off his umbilical hastily. After that, his life had been measured by the oxygen remaining in his suit—fifteen minutes at the most. There were no emergency oxygen bottles to clip on. It wasn't that kind of suit.

His radio had also been wrecked. No chance to signal. Control for a possible rescue launch. Furthermore, the powerful slam of the meteoroid had deflected his ship out of its prescribed orbit. Puzzled radarmen below had seen the blip vanish from their screens. Scanning for it was hopeless as the craft took up a new and random twist through space into a completely unknown and eccentric orbit.

As far as the ground was concerned, the manned vehicle had joined the horde of space debris hurtling around earth at various heights, totaling thousands of pieces, small or large.

But it was one of those maverick pieces of useless junk that now, after the long silence of space, accomplished a reverse miracle. A dead, burned-out comsat, dating back to the early days of space launchings in the 1960's, came angling at the vehicle manned by a frozen corpse. The collision was soundless in the airless void. But pieces of torn metal flew from both. It was a vertical sideswipe that sent the comsat spinning upward in ricochet, the manned craft downward.

Then, in this series of freakish events, another random miracle took place. Deep within the craft's mazes of electronic systems, some circuit had been activated by the jarring impact. Belatedly, computerized tapes fed into the motive power system and retro-rockets thundered silently. The tanks of hypergolic propellants, unaffected by the long dormant stay in space, were still intact and dutifully fed the greedy thrusters.

The frozen man aboard did not care about this untimely release from his eternal orbit among the unblinking stars.

The fully automated system carried on its sequential programming, positioning the heat-shield forward, waiting for the frictional grab of the air to drastically nullify the velocity of 17,000 mph. At the 500-mph point, the braking rockets at the heat-shield's rim burst forth to cushion the final touchdown. All systems had worked. Nothing had been harmed by the meteor except the top-level auto and manual controls, so that only the mid-space collision could jar the slavo-mechanisms into operation. The wreck of the spacecraft settled gently on a glacier.

And so, astronaut Wayne Durk landed after all…

A dead man.

No, not quite a dead man. Slowly his skin warmed, for the glacial cold around him was less than that of space. And by another touch of serendipity, his body unfroze slowly enough to bring recovery. Landing in any hot desert or tropical region, his forced metabolic renewal would have been stoked up fatally.

After a day and night in the subzero temperature, his body had warmed up 400 degrees from its original deep-frozen state. Somewhere along the line, the heart began to beat hesitantly, then more strongly. Lungs began to inhale with infinite slowness but increasing their rhythm in geometric progression. The tingle of life began to suffuse through every dormant organ. The first flush of pink came to the blue skin and dark purple lips.

Last to awaken was the brain, with the ears and open eyes already feeding in stimuli.

Alive, thought Wayne Durk in astonishment.

Alive—but how? The last his fading senses had shown him—and he knew it was the last scene he would ever see again—was the star-sparkled blackness some 650 miles above earth, with the horrifying awareness that he was marooned in space. That only his corpse would continue circuiting earth in his mechanical bier.

Fleetingly, without detail, Durk remembered some space medic's talk, to the effect that there was a remote possibility of an astronaut, if exposed suddenly to space under just the right conditions, not dying. Suspended animation, frozen sleep, cryogenic stasis, call it what you will—he would live. By a second miracle—such as landing in the coldness atop a glacier—he might even revive.

That medic's one-in-a-million prediction had impossibly fulfilled itself.

Alive! Durk's elation abruptly died. It wasn't a miracle, it was a curse.

"It isn't right!" he suddenly yelled aloud. "Why wasn't I allowed to die?" He shook his fist upward, angrily. "Why did I have to be brought back to face… face *it* again? WHY?"

For a moment hope sprang up in him. Maybe he would never make it—being alive. He swayed wildly on his legs on the verge of collapse. An infinite ache throbbed in every bone. No, he wouldn't make it and there was a glad cry in his heart. No man could be frozen solid and then be resurrected, to cheat his grave.

He waited thankfully for delayed death to claim him, once and for all. But he groaned as instead he felt a slow tide of energy rise within him and grow stronger. Soon his rubbery legs were able to support him. Somewhere his helmet had been smashed and knocked off. Panting and wheezing, he drew in the fresh air and lurched toward the hatchway, which was sprung off its hinges and wide open.

Outside, he choked as his lungs drew in the icy air. His gritty eyes took in the giddy sweep from the huge glacier on whose topside he had landed. Durk felt another surge of hope that his life-drama would end the way it should have. He knew he would never make it down the craggy mountain of ice, in his weakened condition.

Somewhere on the way down his feet would slip from under him… he would slide helplessly down the smooth hard whiteness… drop into some deep fissure… his broken body silent at last. He was almost ready to start when he realized what it was… *suicide*.

He drew back. Natural death he could accept, joyfully. But deliberately inviting it, forcing it, *planning* it… no, not that. He cursed the pseudo-religious scruples that had been ingrained in him by his strict Church-going God-worshipping Bible-believing parents. He could no more fight it than… well, than not answering the pangs of hunger and eating.

And that's what he did next, though it was going against himself and his secret wish for oblivion. He dragged himself back into the craft and found a kit of space rations, wolfing them down. He washed it down with water from a canteen.

He wanted to die, and yet he ate to live. Self-preservation. Another of those damnable inbred forces that you couldn't fight, and that was consigning him to the hellishness of life again. Hatefully, he could feel his energy level slowly climbing. But it took another day and night, and more meals, before Durk felt ready to tackle the climb… on the proper terms, not favoring one fate or anther. It was the only way to keep his conscience clear, by striving with all his resources to survive when that was really the last thing he wanted.

What was that old poetic expression? *Man is a fearful and wonderful animal…*

The fearful-wonderful animal had remained in his spacesuit, which superbly insulated him from the arctic air's bite. In fact, his body heat had begun to pile up during the hours before, promising to roast him in layered plastics and aluminum foil. He had had to open his umbilical tube and the cool air that then worked in, plus what seeped down the neck of his suit, served to create a tolerable thermal balance around his skin.

He reviled the spacesuit too. Without it, he would have died of exposure. The accursed thing had further carried on the conspiracy to return him safely to the living.

More practical thoughts forced themselves upon him. Where was he? In Alaska… northern Canada… Siberia? It could be any of the arctic areas that supported unmelting glaciers. Off in the distance he saw snow-tipped mountains, drab forested stretches, desolate snow and ice marching endlessly to the horizon. Obviously, a remote northern land sparsely inhabited, if at all.

Maybe he would end up starving…

He squeezed down the gloating triumph over that thought. Had to play it "straight," he thought. Pretend to want to live and play it for all it was worth. Some things did tug him the other way—seeing his wife and children again, a few friends, his lab staff. His death-wish mellowed somewhat at those thoughts.

And of course he obeyed the rules and strapped the remaining kit of rations and a water canteen over his shoulder. Flinging a last look back at the crumpled spacecraft—how had he survived even that?—Durk began his slippery climb down the glacier. Even though it was tricky work, part of his thoughts went back to his space mission—how long ago? With a start he realized he had no idea how long he had been space frozen.

Days…? Months…? *Years…?*

He dismissed that shocking thought and recalled the roaring launch of the Saturn-nuclear booster that was standard in the 1990's, hurling his one-man laboratory into orbit.

His mission? Why think about it? It had failed…

He was jarred out of his introspection by his feet sliding out from under him, on a smooth patch of glacial ice. Instinctively, clammy fear clutched him as he saw the precipitous edge further on and the sheer drop awaiting him.

Then his mind clicked over and sang. *Over I go, and I can't stop myself. I'm in the clear. I'm not ending it all. I can't help it if there's no way to save myself from a killing drop into an ice crevasse. Soon I'll be released from it all, from having to tell them the bitter news, and from facing IT again.*

Still, half-driven by his hind-brain's brute inheritance to fight for life and his fore-brain's resolve to play the game honestly, his boots and gloved hands clawed uselessly on the sheer smoothness, trying to stop his accelerating slide.

Then, with a half-curse, he saw the patch of dirt that incongruously existed in a hollow of the glacier. In the incredible tenacity of life, scraggly bushes had defiantly taken root.

Involuntary reflexes and voluntary will made him twist and stretch all his agonized muscles in a supreme effort to swing his sliding body close to the patch's edge. His hands grabbed wildly for anything to grip and closed on a thin bush. It gave way, uprooted. But it had slowed his slanting slide and his flailing hands caught hold of another wiry bush—that held.

Ten feet from the man-swallowing gash in the glacier, Durk sat pantingly in the dirt. *I knew it,* he thought wearily. *Another miracle had to shape up and save the life I would rather throw away.*

He had bitterly ridiculous visions of polar-bears dropping dead before they could clutch him, blizzards blowing him straight into an Eskimo village, avalanches backing up for him…

Crazy, wild, his charmed and hated life.

He was not at all surprised to find the rest of his climb down almost effortless, with no further danger. Hand and footholds appeared by enchantment before him. A long gentle slope allowed him to sit and slide on his wear-proof spacesuit's bottom for more than a mile. The edge of the glacier below, where they usually reared in saw-toothed jaggedness, welcomed him with a natural split and a carpet of crushed stone to walk down to solid ground.

And he almost began believing in the intercession of real white-magic when a day later, just as his food and water ran out, two Eskimos driving a snowmobile found him and cheerfully brought him to their village. Durk just knew that here he would find one of the spacetrack stations run by the tribe, who had all the modem paraphernalia known. He was, to all intents and purposes, back in civilization. His trek in the wild was over.

Durk had to put on the proper face for these "saviors" who were exuberantly happy that they had rescued an astronaut from being lost in the wilderness.

He soon indulged in a hot bath and shave. A suit of civvies was requisitioned for him in place of his space-suit, now too hot to wear. The head man of the Eskimo-techs revealed that this was the Alaskan Yukon.

Durk revealed little about himself beyond having been on a presumably routine space mission. He did not want them to know *why* he had been in space, nor what the results had been. That was for Space Security to know first. He was cautiously about to ask for the date, in an offhand manner, when he saw a calendar leaf—May 10, 1998. He had rocketed from earth on May 5, 1997.

He had been space-frozen a year...

CHAPTER 2

Durk was finally flown away in a nuke-flyer. Destination—Province America of the Terran World Union. He braced himself for what he would see, after a year's absence.

Durk was delivered to the Earthia City airport, at his request. He stood for a moment in the terminal, gathering his nerve to face what lay ahead. First, to replug all the circuits of his life. His wish-I-weren't-here-at-all feeling was partly staved by a little glow as he stepped into an optiphone booth, the usual public-service free-of-charge unit.

He buttoned his home and a small eager smile came to his lips. Ellen's dear voice would cheer him up, not to mention Randy's piping and little Wendy's eager treble. God, the kids would be a year older now…

No answer. He frowned in annoyance. The family *would* be out. He started buttoning again, then changed his mind. No, better to walk right in on the chief. Too hard to announce his return, the mission's let-down and all, over the phone. Better to deliver it eyeball to eyeball. He would go there right away.

About to hail an air-taxi, Durk shook his head. On impulse, he decided to walk, at least for a ways. What was the hurry when a year had already slipped down the drain? He stepped toward the motowalks that led out of the airport, then grunted in dismay at the sign on the outer hood—OUT OF ORDER.

This too now? Durk felt his skin crawl. Turning, he saw his reflection in a plate-glass shop window. He stared at himself, the man who had returned from the dead—unwillingly. No, he hadn't changed outwardly. He was still his lanky self, stooped forward a bit as if always bucking a wind. Same generous face—generous nose, large ears, fleshy lips, large-lidded, hazel-green eyes, projecting under jaw. Not handsome, not striking, not arresting, but *powerful*… the reflection of a high-horsepower mind, nine parts genius.

Minds… genius… IQ… the reminder sent a cold wind through his nervous system, colder than the chill arctic air had been.

He plunged forward in a long-strided walk, following the broken-down motowalk out of the airport, to the streets. He took the ramp up to the third level span for a better view of the city. He panned his gaze around and saw no improvement. There was the same air of decay about the city, a slowing down of gears, a gradual but inexorable unwinding of progress.

Durk went in at the third-level span's doorway of the big grey building that housed the Bureau of World Brainpower. The world's brainpower was not in the building, only the low brainpower people who handled and allocated and kept track of top brainpower around the world. He walked down the marbleized hallway and took an elevator up to the 33rd floor. As he stepped out, a formidable security guard blocked his way. But only for a moment. After a quick glance at Durk's face he smiled and backed away.

"How are you, Dr. Durk?" he said in his non-gruff voice, his gruff one being reserved only for unauthorized personnel. "Pass on, sir."

Away a year, no doubt given up for lost in space, and all Breen the guard had to say casually was, "How are you?"

Shaking his head, Durk moved on with the first uneasy feeling of unreality beginning to close in around him. Various clerks and underlings passed him in the long hall of the 33rd floor. They all knew him and flashed him a brief smile, but no one seemed surprised to see him back from the graveyard of space. The feeling of unreality clutched his spine with clammy fingers.

At the door marked—FINNEGAN LLOYD, CHIEF, BWB—Durk walked in without preamble. Miss Petrie, the raven-haired girl secretary, looked up. Her micromini skirt was even shorter than usual, displaying an enticing 90% of her smooth silk-sheathed legs, shapely ones to where they met something brief and frilly. She kept her legs crossed most of the time, out of necessity.

She glanced at Durk rather blankly at first. Ah, he thought, she's going to react now, eyes springing wide as if he were a ghost. But Durk was wrong. Recognition only came into her eyes, no surprise. Her voice was almost scolding. "Dr. Durk, you have no appointment for today."

No appointment? Had everyone gone crazy? Didn't they realize a dead man had walked in? A man who a year before had been launched into oblivion? How could they take his Lazarus-like return so calmly, indifferently?

"I'm sure the chief will want to see me," Durk said in a determined voice. "After all, he never expected I'd walk in again…"

"Uh?" grunted the girl, uncomprehendingly.

"Skip it," snapped Durk, striding to the inner office door.

"You can't disturb him. He's busy…" Miss Petrie had unwrapped her long legs and lunged for him, but Durk shook her off, grasping the door knob. He paused a moment, took a deep breath, and walked in. The chief was in for a shock. Surely he would not, *could* not, react so unconcernedly. Lloyd had been the one who ordered him into space…

The fat balding man at the desk had Ills brows knotted over a brochure, frowning heavily. He did not look up at first. Finnegan Lloyd somehow gave the impression of a chained dynamo instead of a human being. Energy seemed to spill from him and charge the air. The lips of his gash mouth were never still. They constantly twitched, curled, pursed, puckered, twisted, writhed. His eyes were most striking, an intense blue that seemed to send sparkles through the air, as if the brain behind them were a high-voltage machine.

Now those eyes swung on the visitor, with anger. "How did you get past Miss Petrie?" he snarled, his mobile lips flapping out the words forcefully. "I told her I'm too busy to see anyone…" He broke off, taking a full look at the tall lean man waiting expectantly.

The voltage in his eyes dropped perceptibly. Even a faint smile was twistedly fashioned by his lips. "Oh, it's you, Durk. But look, man, I really am busy."

"Busy?" echoed Durk, thunderstruck. For a moment his mouth worked but no words came out. "But chief," he finally croaked, "don't you see who it is? Look at me. I'm back, back from…"

A sharp buzz interrupted. Lloyd leaned over to snap on his optiphone, on which a worried face appeared. Lloyd shot an apologetic look at Durk, lips gyrating. "Important call. Do you mind, old man? Come back later, in a couple hours. Eh?"

Without waiting for an answer, Lloyd turned back to the optiphone and pressed the ready button. The image began to speak in a discouraged mutter.

Standing stunned, Durk wondered if some witch's spell had been cast. *How could Lloyd ignore him, the impossible survivor from space?* Slowly, Durk turned and left the office. Miss Petrie flashed him an uncertain smile, her eyes puzzled, then shrugged and bent over her voicetyper, speaking softly. The clatter of the machine, at the tempo of her fast voice, followed Durk as he went out into the hall and leaned against the wall to collect himself. He really had to collect himself for he felt like a man who had fallen apart with pieces scattered all over.

Something incredible was going on. Something uncanny…

He wasn't ghostly. People did see him, that he knew. He was solid and real—or was he? Durk wasn't even sure at this confused moment. Feeling foolish, he went to the men's room and took a quick look in the mirror. His gaunt face and heavy-lidded eyes stared back at him. The same face he had always had. The face Miss Petrie and Finnegan Lloyd and all the others knew. But a face they hadn't seen for a year. A face they could never have expected to confront them again, after his long sojourn in space on an unscheduled mission—Project Space Corpse. At most, they might have expected to see his frosted face with eyes closed and a death-pallored skin.

Without amusement, Durk thought of that old joke where the fellow said, "Hey, I'm back," to get the scathing answer, "Oh, were you away?"

Durk suddenly craved a smoke. Funny, but his smoking habit had been forgotten since his return to earth. He patted the right pocket of his suitcoat, then remembered he had gotten it from the tech-Eskimos. But he found the money they had thoughtfully put in the pocket.

Taking an elevator down to the lobby, Durk put a plasto-coin in the vending machine that handled all varieties of the weed and a pack of *Grande's* came out. Durk nervously ripped the pliofilm off and thrust a fat cigar into his lips. Two draws and its self-lighting end glowed, sending out curls of smoke.

Durk inhaled it deeply into his lungs, coughing at first, but then feeling the soothing effects as his jangled nerves became lulled by the smoky narcotics. That was one of the few good things in the world to come back to…

Durk gasped a little in surprise. He had almost forgotten about his first reactions to his unwilling earth-return. But that, too, now flooded over him in black tides. *Why didn't I die?* Was joined by *Why isn't anyone surprised I'm back?*

Feeling calmer after puffing the cigar halfway, Durk left the building. The chief had said to be back in a couple hours. He had time to kill. Durk found a street corner optiphone booth and tried calling his home again. Again no answer. Muttering, Durk began walking with another destination in mind. His lab.

Maybe *they*, his staff, would greet him with open arms and bring out the fatted calf. Through long association there was a bond between him and his hard-working crew.

As he walked—it wasn't far—he wondered if any of the frantic lines of research with the Bug had gotten anywhere. The Bug. Anyone passing the tall man would have seen his face turn deadly grim. It was almost a painful explosion of thoughts that were ushered in by the Bug. The Bug had done this to him, in a roundabout way. It had dominated his life, tyrannized him, tormented him for the past ten—no, eleven—years now.

Almost, he turned aside, hating to return to his lab workshop. It loomed more like a torture dungeon in his mind. A labyrinth of maddening riddles and grinding frustrations. That was the main reason he had hated returning to life—because of the Bug.

Durk was too preoccupied to see the huge streamlined truck that bore down on him as he crossed an intersection. The hard metal grill in front raced forward on a direct collision course. With a soft sigh, the electromagnetic cushion gave a little but then halted the grill a yard from Durk. Inside the cab, the driver sat stiffly in his inertia-killing cocoon that had been instantly thrown around him to nullify the abrupt stop. He glared at Durk and yelled "Jaywalker!" Durk glanced at the truck and wished, fervently, that time had turned back a half-century or so, when careless people were killed by roaring vehicles like that.

Even that was denied him, a quick brutal execution by machine.

Ahead he now saw his domed lab, in the Science Park which housed dozens of domes, each a sanctum of a different discipline. It was a complex to which, at one time, any problem could be thrown and this brain mill would crack the nut.

But only half the domes were in operation now—no. Durk's face went ashen as he saw that #47 was now closed with its door barricaded. His eyes swung fearfully. Two others were shut down that had been open a year ago. Durk trembled as if a howling wind were buffeting him.

Since he had been in space, three more labs had closed their doors—forever. Less than half were left now miserable scientific outposts hopelessly making Custer's last stand. He stopped. On one of the abandoned domes had been scrawled, in large misshapen letters—GOOD RIDDANCE, BRAIN-BOYS.

Durk shuddered. It was another sign of something vile and loathsome creeping across the world, the gloating triumph of the normals. The Bug was their ally, their pal, their hero. They cheered its advent and...

With an effort, Durk turned off that horrifying tap of thoughts. He strode toward dome number 3, his lab, not whether he would have been sorry or not, if it too had been bleak and silent. Instead, it was humming in that sound-subliminal way that seemed to exude from any lab, almost as if it were the subtle rustlings of brains at work.

The door's sign said—VIROLOGY LAB. IN CHARGE, DR. WAYNE DURK.

At the door, Durk hesitated, then turned away. In a stab of sympathetic thoughtfulness, he didn't want to barge right in on them. Minor traumas might result in their sensitive minds, at seeing their boss, missing for a year and therefore dead, walking in full of life...

Or would they only turn and smile and go back to work?

Shook up by that possibility, Durk almost began to sneak around the curve of the dome until he came to the large round window through which solar radiation was gathered in certain experiments. He glanced in and felt a momentary glow as he saw old Doc Sawyer bent over his cultures, his straggly goatee almost dipping in the gop… beefy Todd whistling as he waited for the ultracentrifuge to slow down… petite and lovely Trina jabbing at the computer keys daintily but with authority, knowing her business… "Bug boy" Bates peering at the meson-microscope's screen… but that tall stooped figure? A new man?

The figure turned. Durk froze, as rigidly as if he were back in space. He blinked his eyes but the hallucination didn't go away.

How could that man be?

Faintly, Durk heard the bull voice of Henty, the rod-virus specialist, as he said, "Strain 66-B is an abort, Dr. Durk."

The man he called Dr. Durk, looking as if he were always leaning into a wind, only took another puff of his cigar and shrugged eloquently. Watching through the window, Durk could tell the brand of the cigar from its thick shape. *Grande's*, the brand he always smoked…

And in all other ways, *that man in there was his double.*

Not a close double. An *exact* double. Every feature, every line of his body, every expression, every gesture—it was Wayne Durk all over again, in the flesh.

In the flesh? No, how could that be? The dazed mind of the outside Durk tried to rationalize. A robot, an android, some, kind of fake human? Anyway, an *impostor*.

Now, in flashing retrogression, Durk could see why no one had been surprised to see him before. They had thought this fantastic twin of his had walked in, not the Durk who had been lost in space.

As surprise simmered down, anger boiled in Durk. What kind of trick was this? Had the chief done it, and why? Whatever that *thing* in there was, what was its purpose? To keep the staff from knowing their boss was dead, lost in space? But how could any created creature possibly pose as the real thing and convince anybody… no, it didn't make sense. It only made enormous, soul-blasting, brain-searing *nonsense*.

Durk grunted and ran toward the door, seething within. Then he commanded himself to calm down. *Get hold of yourself, boy. Act like a scientist, an intelligent man, not a berserk brute.* There must be some logical reason why his double had been installed in his lab, apparently carrying on his work.

He managed to start opening the door slowly without haste, as he normally would. He wouldn't let this throw him. He would walk in calmly and coolly, keeping his head and his dignity. Then he would politely ask that bogus… that impostor… that counterfeit… that carbon copy… that duplicate… that imitation of himself… to kindly get the hell out while the real thing took over.

With the door only partly open, Durk heard voices drift to him. The other "Durk" was explaining something to several of the staff in the same soft-firm voice Durk would use. It made his skin crawl to hear his own inflections and tonal shades down to the last harmonic and decibel.

Peeking through the half-open door, Durk could also see his double lifting one finger upward in that peculiar gesture he had always used for emphasis. And one eyebrow was uplifted in the typical Durk way when thinking on his feet about some scientific problem, such as they were discussing now.

The voice, the gestures, every little telltale mannerism of Durk was fantastically being exhibited by this… this creature.

Shaken, Durk did not finish opening the door to walk in. He quietly closed it and half-staggered away. It hit him full force that his double could hardly be told from the original. A queer thought ripped through him, taken from an old-time TV show he had read about…

Will the real Wayne Durk please stand up?

CHAPTER 3

Durk's dazed mind noticed it was nightfall. He was in another bar, having his fifth—or was it eighth?—Manhattan. Drink was no answer but he had no other answer to try.

How Durk had obtained the money brought a thin smile to his lips. He had simply signed a money-chit and the bartender had put it through the routine viewer that connected with Central Handwriting Exchange. Naturally, his signature had come out confirmed. That was something his double couldn't quite take away from him, his bank account. At least Durk could draw on it.

One of a parade of *Grande* cigars smoldered in the ashtray. He took a puff but it tasted stale and he flung the butt down in disgust.

He was a ghost, said his befuddled thoughts. A shadow. The skeleton in the family closet. He couldn't even go to his lab and greet his staff. An outcast. An exile. None of them was the right definition for his incredible status, where his damnable double had usurped his life.

He glanced at the clock, startled. He had forgotten but too late to sec the chief now. Besides, he didn't want to report in just now, not while his emotions were all a screeching jangle.

And it did not help to see the news on the wall-TV of the bar. The news told of a crisis in the Terran World Union again, as the General Assembly argued over whether to shift more world brainpower to the Euro Province or the Sov Province. Both were badly in need of science-tech personnel to prevent breakdown of their electropower systems with plants undermanned by competent engineers.

As if to emphasize the lack of such trained minds all over, the TV flickered and a carrier-signal sign immediately flashed on—TECHNICAL TROUBLE, PLEASE STANDBY.

And that reminded Durk of the world he had been forced to return to. A world running down like a clock as the brain gap grew larger and larger... no, he didn't want to think about that. He had enough troubles of his own.

The TV picture returned, with a few more flutters, and showed the newscaster's brittle smile as he said: "The Anti-Brain Movement seems to be spreading, according to recent rumors. Scientists in India have been attacked and beaten up. Laboratory windows were smashed by rocks. It is suspected that an actual international organization has been set up, sworn to take away control of the world from what they call the 'Brainies,' and whom they accuse of causing all the trouble around earth…"

Durk smiled bitterly. They had it all twisted. It was the *lack* of "Brainies" that caused the trouble. What mad things were going on in the world? Where would it all end?

Through the haze in his eyes, Durk saw three burly men enter the bar and look over the patrons searchingly. They were dressed in rough clothing and had hard faces.

Durk suddenly felt a sobering chill as their eyes fastened on him and his neat clothing. They whispered together, pointing at him. Then they sauntered over to him.

"Yer name," snapped one of the men.

Durk was about to answer with dignity but then caught himself. He couldn't say he was Dr. Wayne Durk, not when another man of that name held sway over the virology lab at Science Park. Somehow, it didn't seem right to use that name. Durk fished in his somewhat bleary mind and improvised, "Dan Holton. But what is it to you…"

"Plenty," barked the man, glowering. "You sure you aren't Dr. Wayne Durk? You look like him."

Durk sat up in shock. How would they know him? It was almost as if they had memorized faces and were looking for him. It lanced into his mind—the Anti-Brain Movement.

"Naw, he can't be," mouthed one of the toughies. "No Brainie would lie about it. They're too proud. Forget him."

The other two nodded and with a last scowl at him, they turned to the bar and boisterously ordered drinks. Durk pondered the queer tricks of fate. Ordinarily he would have told his true name and perhaps earned a rough handling by the ABMen. But because his double existed, he had of his own desire given a false name. And saved himself. Within himself, Durk had to laugh. But grindingly. Having a double was worse than any roughing up.

His mind partially cleared by the incident, Durk slapped his half-empty glass on the table and got up to go. Outside, a cool night breeze further swept the cobwebs out of his mind. His step quickened with eagerness.

Home. Ellen and the kids. Stupid of him to sit drinking and brooding over his twin at the lab when he had a wife to return to. Surely she would be home now. Durk hesitated at a street-corner optiphone booth but went on.

His voice over the phone would shock her as much as seeing him in person. Six of one, half dozen of the other.

Durk hailed an airtaxi, having enough money left. Too far to walk to his home, out in Sub city beyond the suburbs. The copter buzzed smoothly through the aerial traffic and beelined for Subcity with its tiers of homes piled high on the plastic rises. Each home was individual with its own plot of ground and artificial sunlight shining down during the day, but all of it stacked up for 100 tiers, pile after pile. Durk wondered how it had been in midcentury times before the population bomb had exploded, when families could actually own a portion of the ground itself. Nobody did anymore except the filthy rich or the string-pullers.

Durk's home was on tier three, itself a mark of his high status as a top scientist. The airtaxi swooped between the tiers and deposited him at the end of the "street." Durk paid and walked toward his white bungalow with green trim, shaped like a pumpkin and rotatable for even day lighting.

His steps became progressively slower. How do you face a wife you haven't seen for a year? What do you say? "Hi, Honey. I'm back. How's things?" But to her he would be a dead man come to life. He had to say something to ease the heart-clutching impact. Like,

"Ellen dear, I'm not dead as they reported… I'm alive."

"Easy, dear girl. Yes, I'm alive after all."

Or the humorous approach? "My death in space was grossly exaggerated."

Damn blast. There *was* no right thing to say. No way to bridge the enormous gap between his being alive and his being absent for a year. And presumed dead, with not much of the "presumed" there.

Walking up to the front door, he braced his shoulders and grasped the doorknob. No, he couldn't walk right in and compound the crisis. Better to ring first and let her open the door. But his finger shook and he pulled it away from the bell button.

Where was she? Was she at ease? Playing with the kids? Feeling like a sneak-thief, he decided to peep in the window first. To do that he would have to step through the shrubbery and glance into the livingroom window. Looking up and down the street to make sure no neighbors would witness his peculiar actions, he stepped through the shrubs to the window.

But before he could raise his face to look in, he heard the soft whir of a car's turboengine. A startled glance over his shoulder showed the car turning into his drive, having taken the ramp approach to tier three. It was a sporty Orion, the same car he had had a year ago, with a slight dent in its front left fender.

Durk stood rooted, feeling nightmarish unreality steal over him again. The car stopped and out stepped Dr. Durk—the other one. Durk panted hoarsely, disbelieving his eyes.

His lab *and* his home? Durk hadn't been prepared for this unthinkable extension of his double's role. Why, this was taking over his whole *life*...

It was like an impossible dream. Durk remained hidden by the shrubs and watched his other self march up the steps and open the door with all the familiarity of a man coming home to his family.

How *dare he? How dare he do this vile thing?* Rage made a tempest in Durk and he almost darted forth, except that his knees felt so weak he couldn't move. The door swung open and the other Durk stepped in. Ellen came smiling to greet him. Through the open door, Durk saw her arms entwine the man who entered. It was the embrace of a loving wife.

Atrocity piled on atrocity as a boy and girl came running with childish cries, throwing themselves at their daddy.

Watching, Durk was scarcely able to suppress his inward moans. This bogus Durk was stealing all the warmth and affection that he, the real Durk, should be getting. It was thievery worse than if he had stolen a fortune from Durk.

But another horrifying thought exploded in Durk's mind, like a bomb. *How could Ellen and the children be fooled?* They knew his every last little mannerism, his slightest twitch of the lips when talking, the subtly changing expressions in his eyes. No one could possibly imitate a man's full repertory of individual characteristics enough to deceive those with whom he lived in intimate daily life.

Then how could they take this fraudulent Durk for the real one?

Durk's whole world was tumbling down around him. There was only one insane, inconceivable answer—the other Durk was an exact *carbon copy.* Not only his outward double but his inward double. He must possess every memory Durk himself ever had. Must think precisely like Durk. Must unconsciously act like Durk under any and all circumstances. A puppet who was as real as his master. The inevitable conclusion to it all seared its way into Durk's gibbering thoughts...

The second Durk must believe he IS Durk.

Swept away were all possibilities of clever androids or trained robots, or any other lab-made duplicates. The double was not only a flesh-and-blood but brain-and-thought facsimile of Durk, down to the last cell and convolution of the brain.

Yet how could that be? Where had he come from?

Durk told himself not to do it. That it would only add to his already unbearable torment. But he could not fight the impulse to slowly raise his head, from his position behind the shrubbery, and look into the livingroom window.

It was like *déjà-vu*, that strange feeling of having lived a scene before. There sat his usurper sipping a cocktail with Ellen, smiling in each other's eyes. Then he leaned forward to scoop up cheese dip with a potato chip, holding it up first and licking his lips ostentatiously. Then he gobbled it down in one gulp, with bulging eyes to the tune of peals of laughter from the kids.

Durk's eyes rolled. It was all done the way he had always done it, as a sort of family ritual. Down to every last gesture and facetious expression. No other man could have imitated that simple, but incredibly complex, series of little movements and facial distortions, ever. No man but Durk, the true Durk, could do it.

How could his double be so REAL?

Durk's mind swam in a foggy sea of incomprehension and disbelief. It was as if he had died and been reincarnated in his exact likeness. A sudden occult fear stabbed through Durk. Had he somehow died out in space, without knowing it? And then had eerie forces replaced him physically on earth?

He shook that mad thought out of his head, with all the previous evidence that people saw him and that he was tangible and living.

Now Randy, age 10, was proudly showing his "daddy" how he could punch out answers on his toy computer. A toy that was equal to big computers of mid-century times. Then little five-year-old Wendy took a running leap into his arms, her pigtails flying. With a happy smile creasing her chubby face, she planted a wet kiss on his lips, representing the magic love of a child for its father…

But Durk wasn't watching anymore. He couldn't take it. He had slid down nervelessly, fighting to keep from screaming aloud. This abominable farce had to end. It was sacrilege for a man's diabolical double to play the part of the real man of that household, under false pretenses, and to reap all the love rewards.

Durk began to bundle up his shaking nerves. It had to be done now. But not in anger or bitter denunciation. It had to be in a gentlemanly way so as not to alarm Ellen and the kids more than necessary.

He would ring the bell, then walk in calmly. "Sir," he would say politely, "I'm Dr. Wayne Durk. The original one. The one and only. Whoever or whatever you are, I request that you step out of my life and…"

Rot. That would be ridiculous. No, he would have to march in boldly, somewhat incensed, since he had a right to be, and firmly declare: "Now look here. Take a look and you'll see I'm *the* Dr. Durk. How this happened I don't know but out—out! Hear me? Explanations can come later and..."

Durk kept on fantasizing in a dozen other ways. But it wouldn't matter what he'd say. The stark picture rose in his mind of Ellen staring with widening eyes at the two men, as alike as peas in a pod. A hand would go to her mouth to stop a scream. Randy and Wendy... their little hearts would beat in fright, fright at the sight of two identical daddies, their loyalty already torn...

No, no. Durk saw it was impossible to walk in and blight the lives of the ones he loved, irrevocably. The trauma would give their loving hearts and tender minds a mortal wound for life. The situation had to be resolved some other way. In private, between him and the Durk double. Then the other Durk could walk away, never to return.

Another curious thought speared its way into Durk's mind. How soon had the double showed up, after his fatal spaceflight? *The next day, maybe?* In that case, Ellen and the kids had never suffered the loss of a husband and father. And if Durk walked in, claiming he was back from the dead, they would think *he* was the impostor...

Durk gave it up with a silent groan. Wearily, feeling as if he had gone through purgatory, he crept out from the shrubbery and slowly shuffled down the street, shoulders bent. Whatever the answer was to the agonizing mystery, Durk could see nothing but blackness ahead in his life.

A double was not just double trouble. It leaped geometrically by magnitudes into macro-trouble beyond the human capacity to deal with it.

His chief at BWB, Finnegan Lloyd, must know something of this. He would see him first thing in the morning. For the rest of that night, Durk was a lone figure wandering through the darkened city, staring at the stars in silent appeal at times.

CHAPTER 4

"Come in, Durk," said Finnegan Lloyd in his dynamic voice that seemed to sizzle through the air. "What can I do for you at this early hour? You never came back yesterday, you know."

Durk spoke slowly. He had rehearsed it all night.

"Brace yourself, chief. I'm the real Durk…"

He spoke so slowly that Lloyd interrupted. "Well, of course you're Durk. Nobody questioned your identity or suspected you were a spy." He went on bustlingly. "Well, what is it, man? Something wrong at the lab? Short of supplies? Anything else you need?"

"Yes," said Durk in almost a sepulchral voice, "I need my identity back. My status, my lab, my home… my life. It's all been robbed from me."

"Durk; what are you—" Lloyd suddenly peered closely at Durk's haggard face and smoldering eyes. "Wait… *who are you?*"

A faint smile tugged at Durk's lips. "Ah, so it's coming to you now, who I am. I'm the Wayne Durk who went on a special space mission on May 5, 1997, a year ago, and never came back—until now."

Finnegan Lloyd stared like a frozen statue with its mouth open. The shock in his eyes almost shone out like a beacon. Finally, he moved—quickly. He went to the door and pulled the security lever that made it unopenable from the other side. Then he lumbered his fat body to the window and clamped it shut. After unplugging the phone and recorder unit, and glancing around the room as if to make sure no spies were lurking under the furniture, he faced Durk.

"You survived," he whispered, awed. "And returned. How?"

Briefly, biting off the words tersely, Durk told his story.

"A blasted miracle," murmured Lloyd. By the tremor of his hands he was still shaken by this real-life apparition. "We never expected you to come back alive, after we lost track of your spacecraft." He brightened and became hearty, but in a forced way as if unwillingly. He stuck out a hand. "Glad you're back, Durk. Wonderful to find you alive…"

"Cut the phony gladhand," hissed Durk, seething within. "I want to know only one thing—*who's that man in my place?*"

"Oh, you mean—" stammered Lloyd, now thoroughly flustered.

"Yes, I mean that other Dr. Durk. My double. The one who took over my lab and my home and kisses my wife—" Durk kept control of himself with an effort. But there was still a hysterical edge to his voice as he went on. "He's as much like me as I am myself. If I were shaving his face in the mirror I wouldn't know the difference. He's me, inside and out. And even up here." Durk tapped his head. "Now explain, if you know about it." His voice rose almost to a shout.

The chief of world brainpower put a soothing hand on Durk's arm. "Take it easy, man. I'll explain." He gave Durk an appraising glance. "But it's going to be hard for you to take."

"Give," yelled Durk, shaking off his hand roughly. "I want to hear the whole bloody thing from start to finish."

"Sit down," invited Lloyd, plopping himself into his own cushioned chair behind his desk. Durk complied, tensely, sitting like a coiled spring.

Lloyd picked up a pencil and fiddled with it, nervously. "First of all, Durk, we didn't *know* you'd come back some day. We thought you were gone for good and…"

"Skip the apologies and all that rot," snapped Durk, his dark eyes compellingly on his chief.

Lloyd abruptly changed the subject. "Remember before you went up in the rocket, the thorough physical we gave you? You thought it was a routine but we made a tape of you."

"Tape?" echoed Durk blankly. "Of my voice?"

"Not your voice," mumbled Lloyd as if uncertain how to go on. "A different kind of tape that—" He stopped and bounced to his feet. "Oh, hell. I can't give it to you cold. Come with me and you'll see the whole thing before your eyes."

Mystified, and more calm now, Durk arose and followed the fat man out of the office. Lloyd whispered a few words to his secretary, and she hastily grabbed up the telephone.

Lloyd beckoned Durk out into the hallway and down the corridor to an elevator. But it was set apart from the other public elevators. Also a guard stood there, who moved aside as Lloyd waved. Durk saw with growing wonder that Lloyd used a key to open the doors before they could step in. Lloyd kept silent as the cage plummeted down for 33 floors—and kept going down. Durk could sense that, though no indicator in the elevator revealed the floors. Obviously, Durk sensed, he was being let into something top secret.

Something far underground.

The doors opened and they stepped out into a concrete hall, this time facing three guards, heavily armed. They were security guards of the BWB by their arm insignia.

"Your ID, sir," said one respectfully but firmly.

Durk expected Lloyd to burst out in fury at his identity being questioned but instead, he meekly held out a metallic pass. The guard nodded and stood aside. Their footsteps clattered down the concrete hallway which ended in a solid steel door flanked by two guards. They saluted the chief, obviously having been informed by intercom that he was coming, and swung open the massive door.

Durk gasped at what lay beyond. It was the beginning vista of a gigantic hospital system, interspersed with labs and computers that they walked past. White-robed medical men and nurses moved around among scientists in lab-coats. The hum of various electronic devices and other apparatus filled the air.

"What is this place?" demanded Durk, his curiosity at the bursting point. "I never saw it before or even heard of it."

"Built while you were lost in space," said Lloyd.

"Name?"

A slight hesitation, then: "Recreate Labs."

"Recreate?"

"Patience, man. You'll find out what it means."

Durk subsided, satisfied that soon he would be given an explanation for being identical twins instead of one person. But somehow, at the same time, he dreaded the revelation.

Lloyd led the way into a chamber where a huge computer complex filled most of the room. A man was lying naked on a cot in a plastic cabinet. A boxlike ray-projector shone spangled beams which played up and down his body, from top to toe, in a rhythmic cadence. Back and forth, steadily.

Oddly, it reminded Durk of a TV-camera scanning, or panning, the target object. Durk made a startled exclamation, peering through the transparent cabinet.

"Why, that's Dr. Eng of the Sino Province. Top-notch nuclear scientist. What's he doing here on this side of the world, in that queer cabinet?"

Lloyd didn't answer but called over a lab-smocked man whom Durk also knew, surprised. "Doctor Hazen, who gave me my physical before I was launched a year ago." Lloyd whispered in Hazen's ear and the latter's eyes grew round as he stared at Durk. "Dr. Durk," said Hazen and his voice held something like awe. "The man who came back from space alive. And the first man to have a recreate…"

Lloyd kicked him and he coughed, starting again. "Durk, I'm going to explain something utterly unique to you. Something that will be a total surprise. When we gave you that physical exam before your flight, you were blacked out for a while. Remember?"

Durk nodded. "You gave me pentothol. Told me it was to tone me up."

"Actually, you were put in there." Hazen pointed at the man in the cabinet.

"Why?" said Durk, puzzled.

"To have your life-tape made."

"Life-tape?"

Hazen took a breath. "A tape-recorder makes a magnetic record on a tape. Your voice can then be played back. A computer-tape can likewise be replayed. A video-tape's playback recreates a TV program in its entirety."

Hazen tried to be academically nonchalant as he waved at the man in the cabinet. "That scan-ray uses neutrinos, the subatomic particles that can penetrate matter far more easily than X-rays. The focused N-ray is scanning the man's whole physical body, layer by layer from the skin inward, down to the last cell and atom. It makes a permanent record of the man. But not only his body. There is a neuro-encephalic attachment that records his brain-waves, his nerve currents, his cranial convolutions. It 'dissects' the brain, so to speak, and is even able to record all his memory patterns imprinted within the cortex's memory-banks, to use a cybernetic term."

Durk was thinking fast, and thinking ahead, and the pallor of his skin became slowly grey. "Every cell of the body. Every part of the brain. Every memory and nerve-circuit and neuropathic function. Why—that's the *complete* man!"

Lloyd and Hazen stared at Durk, as if waiting for him to go on with the rest, to the incredible denouement. But Durk didn't dare. It was *too* incredible. He shook his head dumbly, his lips twitching uncontrollably.

Hazen said no more but stepped away to where technicians were handling controls. The scanner-ray in the cabinet cut off. Hazen lifted a lid and took out a reel of peculiar tape that seemed rubbery in texture. With the reel under his arm he waved silently for Durk and Lloyd to follow him into the next chamber.

Durk's legs moved in a dreamlike state. He knew what was coming and yet he refused to allow the horrendous thought to come to the surface of his mind. His lanky body stiffened as he watched Hazen put the reel of tape into a computer-like apparatus. The reel began to turn, slowly.

Hazen pointed at a large plastic jar eight feet high. At the bottom was a mirror somewhat like a telescopic lens. The mirror glowed phosphorescently but Durk knew it was nuclear radiation of some sort. Connected to the big jar was a hose that led to a metal tank surrounded by giant magnets.

As technicians worked controls, a misty substance that reminded Durk of ectoplasm in spirit photographs was piped into the jar.

"That tank is a magnetic sink of enormous gauss power which holds energy, from nuclear reactions, in suspension. The energy is being piped into the jar where it will be congealed into matter."

The old Einsteinian bit, thought Durk—matter into energy and vice versa. Rather startling on such a large scale yet nothing new. But if it were *living* matter...

Durk broke off his premonitions, his breath increasing to a pant.

"Under the influence of that neutrino-mirror in the jar," went on Hazen pedantically, "atoms are created in a precise pattern determined by the playback of the life-tape. Observe."

Within the jar, Durk saw the swirling ectoplasmic energy becoming thicker and congealing. He had a swift sense of a human body being built up from the bones outward. There were brief glimpses of tissue forming, muscles, nerve networks, layers of skin. Yet it was all a swift blur.

"Just as a TV image is built up of lines forming rapidly into a picture, the life-tape builds up an organism layer by layer. But just as rapidly in the realm of electronic time, measured in nanoseconds or less."

Durk's throat was dry. His tongue made meaningless sounds at what materialized there in the plastic jar—a naked man.

A naked man who was the double of—

"Dr. Eng!" said Durk hoarsely. "Is it... he, alive?"

CHAPTER 5

"Not yet," said Dr. Hazen softly. "We have to put him through a revitalization process. Starting up his heart and lungs, jogging his glands, that sort of thing. Like spanking a newborn baby to make it start breathing. And it will actually be his 'birth' into the living world."

Finnegan Lloyd turned to look squarely in Durk's eyes. "Now you see?"

Durk couldn't hold back the torrent of awareness anymore in his mind which had integrated all he had seen and heard. Strangely, a calm had come over him.

"Yes, I see. You made a life-tape of me before I was launched. Then, when I seemed lost in space, you took out my life-tape and recreated me, in that plastic jar. Just as you did Dr. Eng."

He raised weary-wise eyes that seemed to have looked into a forbidden place. "The recreate—as you call it—is the *identical* double of the original man. Not only the same physical body, made of new matter, but the same brain and mind and memory and habits and characteristics and personality. Down to the last psychic drop." Lloyd spoke gently. "A shocker, no doubt about that. The Durk recreate is *you*. There is no slightest difference between you."

Durk accepted that with no more than a gust of emotional wind that seized him briefly and let him go. "When was my double... uh... created?"

"Four days after your launching and three days after your spacecraft was lost to tracking. We figured according to available oxygen that you could not possibly live longer than that."

Durk grinned ghoulishly. "Then I've got one thing my recreate hasn't got," he said maliciously. "Memory of what happened in space. There must be a gap in his memory then, from the moment I had my physical when my life-tape was made, and the day he was created."

Lloyd nodded. "Outside of that he has all your memories, clear back to childhood."

A bizarre thought struck Durk. "Does my recreate believe *he* is the one and only Dr. Durk?"

Lloyd looked as if he wished he were far away. "Yes."

"In other words, you didn't tell him he was a recreate?"

"No, Durk. But be reasonable, man. It was only because you were dead at the time. Presumed dead, that is. We saw no reason to acquaint him with the fact that you were lost in space and that he was a copy of you. What would have been the good of it?"

Durk nodded, conceding the point. "But what about the others, where the original man and recreate are both alive?"

"There of course we simply tell the recreate the truth. It shakes them for a moment because you see they feel as if they really existed a lifetime. They have all the childhood memories of the original man. They remember their marriage, the kids coming along, everything. So when we tell them they are newly created and haven't really lived before, it does cause some confusion and adjustment in their minds. They know that the wife and kids they think they lived with have never seen them. They start on a new life of their own."

"Except in the case of my recreate," muttered Durk darkly. "He took over my life."

Lloyd looked pained. "I told you…"

"Yes, I know. You thought the original was gone forever so why not let the recreate take my place in full—" He stopped in shock. "What about Ellen and the kids? Do they know?"

"No. It seemed wiser to let her think it was her own husband."

Yes, reflected Durk bitterly. How could she live with a *substitute?*

Lloyd went on half-pleadingly. "In fact, Durk, we did it out of kindness to her. Your recreate was the first of all. Since it came out successfully, we immediately saw how we could spare her the agony of losing a husband."

"But how did you cover up my 'return' from space after I had been lost?"

"She never knew you were lost. That was kept in security wraps. After your recreate came alive and was given the cover-up explanation we devised, he simply told her—and believed it—that his space mission had been a violent abort, accounting for his absence for a while, recuperating in a hospital. It all fit in, you see. Ellen accepted it without suspicion."

Obviously she would, Durk thought. She could plainly *see* her man was back, safe and sound. The same voice, the same twinkle in the eye at times, the same sudden-fierce embrace…

Durk winced. But philosophical calm still held him. "Your point in all this making of recreates is to replenish the world brainbank?"

"Naturally," said Lloyd, and there was hopefulness in his voice. "It's the only way we have for fighting the brain drain. If we can't lick the Bug, we can at least try to keep up with its depredations. We haven't caught up with the death rate yet but we can in time. We can recreate all the scientists and high-IQ people on earth, eventually."

"Over and over?" asked Durk with a catch in his breath at that sudden new angle to this whole weird business.

Lloyd shook his head. "It seems the life-tape only works well the first time. When we try a second recreate of the same man, it comes out... ah... quite distorted. And dead, fortunately."

"But you could make a new life-tape of the same man and from that get a second perfect recreate?"

"Heaven forbid," said Lloyd fervently. "It's trouble enough explaining to one recreate why he can't go home and sleep with the women he—or his original—married." His fat face was a bit haggard. "The past year, since we began the recreations starting with you, hasn't been exactly fun for me. The burden of this whole project has fallen on me, as chief of world brainpower."

"How many have followed me?" said Durk curiously.

"We've been stepping up the recreate process to 20 a day so far. I think Dr. Eng was number 6899 after you. 6899 headaches..."

Durk could well imagine. 6899 recreated human beings, with all the temperamental traits of their originals—stubbornness, pride, jealousy, love and hatred. He did not envy Lloyd, briefing each one as to his birth out of a life-tape, smoothing down the emotional storms, waiting for their resigned acceptance, then sending them on their way with a pat on the back.

"Some of them disbelieved me," Lloyd was muttering, his fat face quivering. "Accused me of concocting a crazy story and all that. Then the only thing to do was to have the original walk in and face them, eyeball to eyeball. A shocking way to do it. One of the recreates went insane on the spot..."

Lloyd ran his paw over his jowled face, then looked at Durk with sudden eagerness. "But we can end all that travail if your space mission was successful. You haven't told me yet. Did you find the Bug out there?"

Durk hated to answer as he saw the hopeful appeal in his chief's face. "Not a trace, chief. I'm sorry. Mission a failure."

Lloyd said nothing. He just suddenly looked twenty years older. "I was afraid to ask before," he whispered. "Afraid of that answer. Well, you'll have an official debriefing this afternoon. I already had my secretary make the arrangements. Come on, let's go."

As they strode through the next chamber, another man lay naked in the plastic cabinet, with the neutrino scanner swinging back and forth methodically, recording his body and mind to the last detail. Then another man created in a non-Biblical way would open his eyes and think he had been born of woman...

But his shock at the truth later could hardly be any greater than the staggering impact of what Durk had felt, from the other side of the fence. So here he was, a double man… identical twins… and even God couldn't tell them apart.

Durk could hold back the nagging thought no longer, the one that was churning up his insides. In the elevator going up, he fiercely grabbed Lloyd's arm.

"Now the jackpot question, chief. *Which one of us—my recreate or me—will continue as Dr. Wayne Durk?*"

Lloyd's face became ashen. "I was hoping you wouldn't ask that question just yet. Lord, man. How should I know? In the other cases, there was no problem. The recreate had to find his own life. But in your case, where your double has taken up your life…" He spread his hands helplessly. "I'm not Solomon. It will have to be settled later, Durk, after due thought. Meanwhile, of course, we keep your return top secret. You haven't told anyone else?"

"Not a soul," Durk said, reliving those ghastly moments at the lab when he had finally turned away, and at home, when he could not bring himself to reveal his return from the dead to his wife.

How could be EVER do it?

* * * *

"Gentlemen," said Finnegan Lloyd crisply, his charged personality filling the conference room. "You are all sworn to secrecy over what will be revealed to you. It involves security in relationship to Brain Virus IQ—the Bug, in short."

The three men, one in military uniform, stared back stonily.

"You hardly need to tell us that," snapped Marshall Quinby A. Todd, testily. "We're aware of the situation. I represent Space Security and all that it implies. We certainly don't want it bruited about that our launch sent a brilliant scientist—one of the few left—to his seeming doom."

"That isn't the point," spoke up a mousy civilian shrilly, with a mustache that quivered. He was Josas de Milleaux, head of the Brain Virus Commission of the Terran World Union. "Nobody is going to censure the military for an unforeseen space accident. The point is whether Dr. Durk, the world's leading virologist, brought back any clue to the BV-IQ."

"And if he did," came the stolid voice of Leonid V. Stokov, a burly man who headed the World Security Police, "we must keep the news from the Anti-Brain Movement. Another good reason for absolute security."

They all turned to look at Durk now, awaiting his answer.

"Space mission negative," he said tersely, wasting no time.

Their faces registered resignation as though they had not held out much hope anyway.

"There is no slightest trace of the BV-IQ in orbital space, not even in spore form. I had enough time before my accident to determine that by taking in periodic samples of the space environment—vacuum samples if you will—to find them sterile. Also, the Benda-Holt chromatascopic detector showed no organic matter of any kind in wide sweeps around my spacecraft. My polar orbit gave me complete coverage of earth's vicinity each day at heights varying from 100 to 500 miles. It is inconceivable that the virus could lurk higher and then somehow dart down to earth without contaminating the lower region that I surveyed. The report must be unequivocally negative as to the BV-IQ drifting in from outer space."

Milleaux sprang to his feet, exasperated. "But the BV-IQ has never been detected in earth's air either. If it is not transmitted through the air, and doesn't filter down from space, then how can it be *contagious?*"

He glared around challengingly.

Durk answered for them all. "That is the paradox. We have a worldwide epidemic of brain-rot disease that suddenly sprang up 11 years ago. It displayed all the classical symptoms of a contagious plague, like bubonic, that was being spread from victim to victim. Yet we have found no mechanism whereby that could occur. The BV-IQ 'Bug' is not transmitted through the air, or food, or water, or even feces. All of these possibilities have been checked thoroughly."

His voice took on a note of the frustration that all bioscientists felt. "So we have a medical mystery of deadly scope. Somehow, the virus abruptly appears in a new victim's brain, literally out of nowhere, and turns his cerebral organ into rotted matter within three days. The worst of it is, we have no cure, no anti-toxin, no preventative. The death-rate percentage, for the first time in medical history, is 100%. Every stricken victim dies without fail."

CHAPTER 6

Durk paused, overwhelmed himself by this reiteration of an impossibly effective epidemic disease.

"The other mystery is even greater," shrilled Milleaux, waving his arms for emphasis. "Why has the brain virus earned its designation 'IQ' by attacking only men having an IQ of 125 and higher, into the genius range? Why does it selectively leave entirely untouched all those with an IQ below 125? It is like the devil himself at work."

Durk responded at the clinical level, avoiding the more alarming implications.

"Very highly specialized and peculiar viruses or germs have been known before. There is a virus, for instance, that attacks only mollusks. Another that preys only on the eye-tissues of reptiles. Then there is the malaria germ which breeds only within the life-cycle of Anopheles mosquitoes and is thus transmitted to man. This shows how selective viruses and germs can be. And in the case of BV-IQ, we have some faint indications that it can feed only on brains with the increased bio-electric currents that flow within a high-IQ organ. Duller brains with a lesser flow of bionic energy do not tempt them."

"That still does not explain how the virus skips from one high-powered brain to the next." Marshall Todd whiplashed out the words, impatiently. "Isn't *that* what you have to know before you can lick an epidemic?"

"And if we don't lick it," put in Milleaux impulsively, using the English idiom of which he was proud, "*we're* licked. The human race. Civilization. The works."

They all pondered that grim *sequitur*, gravely.

Durk faced Josas de Milleaux. "Sir, just how bad is the situation now? I've been gone, as you know, for a year."

"How bad? Bad bad," spat out Milleaux. "I have some statistics—" He fumbled some crumpled papers out of his crumpled suit. "Here they are. In the industrial area, over 10,000 firms have gone bankrupt for lack of good business executives. Automation has broken down in 50,000 worldwide factories, lacking engineering staffs of high caliber. International finance has had three crises and the stock market collapsed twice, with financial geniuses steadily dying from brain-rot. In the science field, over 100,000 labs have been shut down as talent died off."

He peered at another paper and glanced up ominously. "Brace yourself, Dr. Durk. There are less than ten million scientists left on earth today."

An infinite ache throbbed in Durk's brain.

There had been twenty-five million worldwide scientists 11 years ago. The brain blight had wiped out more than half the world's laboratory brain-power.

"Furthermore," went on Milleaux inexorably, "there is no scientist left with an IQ higher than 155."

Lloyd leaned over and whispered in the Frenchman's ear.

"With one exception," said Milleaux with an odd leer. "Your IQ, Dr. Durk, is 157. That makes you the brainiest scientist on earth today."

All eyes turned to Durk but he was too stunned to blush. All top-grade genius on earth killed off already, promoting his lesser-grade genius to the number one spot. That, to Durk, was the most vivid and frightful sign of how the brain blight was slowly strangling civilization. How could a world built by class-A science-technology brains be run by class-B brains? Durk had no personal illusions on that score. He was an "Einstein" by default only. He was not in the big leagues with the former IQ's that had soared up to 200.

And now the world had to depend on him and lesser intellects, to stave off the collapse of civilization as known on earth. If class-A minds had been wiped out to the same degree in all other fields—industry, academics, engineering, invention, education—then the handwriting was on the wall.

And government too. It was known even a year ago that the Terran World Government was being infiltrated—quite out of necessity—by incompetents. The present World President, by all standards, was near to being a numbskull.

The "collapse" of civilization was an unexaggerated threat. Civilization in the machine sense had always depended, all through history, on the comparatively few science-tech minds that had devised it, kept it going, and improved it. Without that group, the rest of average-brained humanity was helpless to work computers, run experiments, or repair intricate electronic equipment. Engineering science in large part kept the wheels going. Deterioration was inevitable without top talent in charge to *supervise*.

That was the crux of it. Executives, decision-makers, order-givers. These had to be top-rank too, in any area of the civilized arena. With that high IQ reservoir being drained away, the world would eventually be *leaderless*. No culture based on a technical webwork could survive that.

Durk found himself cursing fate again for fishing him out of death's pool and sending him back to a dying world. It was not a pretty sight to see civilization slowly crumbling, falling apart bit by bit. Ten years of decline around him had marked his soul with erosive sadness.

Josas de Milleaux gave the keynote of the meeting, before it broke up. "Dr. Durk's space mission was really a success," he said solemnly. "Successful in proving we can't stop the Brain Bug, at least in the foreseeable future. Therefore, our recreate program is our only hope. We must step up operations until the 'birth' rate of recreates equals the death rate of scientists."

Finnegan Lloyd spoke up eagerly. Too eagerly, Durk thought.

"And I suggest that since Dr. Durk's recreate is working as hard as he can on the pathological end of it, Dr. Durk himself be placed in charge of the recreate program. Then we'll have the two most brilliant men on earth doing the two most important jobs."

Lloyd beamed at his clever summary. Durk glared at him, overwhelmed at the sudden proposal. But the others instantly smiled, taking Lloyd's idea as a stroke of genius.

"Agreed," they murmured, turning to leave.

Lloyd turned to Durk. "There's the answer to your question. Partially, anyway. Your recreate is to continue as Dr. Durk at the virus lab. You will have the new job." He went on hurriedly. "Now, we'll start making plans right away for stepping up the recreate program…"

"And just how," interrupted Durk icily, "does that settle my problem of which Durk goes *home* at night? To Ellen and the kids?"

Lloyd sighed and rolled his eyes. Suddenly he stiffened. "I've been thinking and I've got to give it to you straight. There would be no way for you to resume your home life without telling your double first. Then, assuming he agrees, you could quietly slip into his place at home from then on." Lloyd held up a hand at the sudden brightening look in Durk's face. "But then, what happens? The other Durk has a *year of memory* that you haven't got. Memories he and Ellen alone share. Little things, like that day with the kids at the amusement park… a quiet dinner out and alone… the night you came home beat from the lab and snarled about the damned Bug. Things like that."

Durk was sagging. Lloyd went on relentlessly. "Sooner or later you would slip. You wouldn't remember something and Ellen's suspicions would flame. She would begin to add up the little discrepancies. And then, one day, she would know the *wrong* man—to *her*—was in the house. Don't you see, Durk?"

Yes, Durk could see. He, the real Durk, would paradoxically be exposed as the "impostor" in Ellen's eyes. He could already picture the spreading horror in her eyes as she looked upon him as an *alien* in her home. A false Durk, an intruder, a deceiver.

And if he then hastily explained about the recreate process, she would suddenly understand—and her thoughts would have to make a complete and agonizing about-face. She would realize in one frightful upheaval that she had really been *living* with the "impostor" for a whole year, without knowing. That second shock would be even worse than the first.

Durk's body jerked as if he were being buffeted by gusts of hurricane violence. Greater forces than he could muster had taken over his life, making a mockery of his past and a farce of his future.

He came to the inevitable and inescapable conclusion. "You win, chief. I'll take the new job. Do me a favor. Make it an order so I won't have to believe I made the decision myself."

He managed a ghastly grin that made Lloyd wish the Bug had gotten him. Lloyd put a hand on Durk's arm, his voice low, tense. "For whatever it's worth, you and your recreate may beat the Bug and"—he hesitated—"save the world."

At that moment, Durk couldn't have cared less.

* * * *

Just one hour, thought Durk. One measly little, heavenly hour with them. It wouldn't hurt. He took out his key—he still had his own—and opened the front door, quietly. He tiptoed into the kitchen.

There was Ellen, dear Ellen, her back turned as she whipped a cake batter. Her blond hair tossed as she increased her tempo. Durk could see part of her profile, the same pert nose, full sweet lips, softly rounded chin that he loved to chuck.

Telling his heartbeat to quiet down below 200, Durk tiptoed forward and slipped his arms around her.

"Oh," she said startled, half fearfully.

He gave her the sudden-fierce embrace. Then she relaxed, without turning. "Oh, you goof, always sneaking up on me." Then she wriggled loose from his arms and turned. "But why are you home early from the lab, darling?"

"Got an hour off," said Durk airily. "Nothing but routine culture blob samples and oven tests. Just decided to amble home and find out what a mess you always have the house in when I'm not around."

He frowned at her in mock accusation.

"Oh, you!" She patted his cheek. "The house isn't in a mess, but I am." With a little shriek, glancing in a mirror hung on the door, she scampered from the room. "Give me a minute to change from a scullery maid to a queen," her voice drifted back.

Durk wandered into the livingroom, drinking in the old familiar sights and feelings. Their comfortable sanctuary, hallowed by a trusting love. Even the spot on the carpeting, where he had once spilled some ink, was a fond memory of the past. The furniture had new slipcovers but then Ellen had needed them, a year ago.

A year. A full year since he had slumped into the over-stuffed chair, his favorite. His face clouded. A year while his double had lounged here in his place, usurping the marital bliss that was rightfully Durk's. And if there had been any unbliss… well, it served him right.

Ellen swept in, her attire completely changed, her face made up taste-fully, and her hair neatly combed and tucked. Durk stared, in undisguised admiration. Ellen gave him a flirting look. "Notice the special thing I'm wearing, dear?"

Durk looked over her blankly, and stopped breathing.

"You know, the gift you bought me last month?"

"Last month," muttered Durk, in growing panic.

Ellen's smile began to fade a little. "You couldn't have forgotten, dar-ling. You said they matched my sparkling eyes. Don't you remember—?"

Durk passed a hand over his brow, trying to look weary. "So many dis-tracting things at the lab… experiments going wrong… all that."

"I understand, dear," said Ellen quickly, but with a puzzled glance at him. Then she wiggled at her ears. "This pair of sapphire earrings, silly."

"Oh, yes. Yes of course." Durk slapped his forehead in recrimination. "And they do match your beautiful eyes, you witch."

He tried to cover up the awkward moment by leaping to his feet to clutch her. But two piping voices pealed out as the door banged open and two small forms came dancing in.

"Daddy! Daddy's home!" Little Wendy got there first and took a running leap into Durk's ready arms. That he remembered all too well. He swept her up and dangled her near the ceiling, shaking her until she squealed in de-light. Then he tossed her on the sofa and quickly turned to stoop and grab Randy in the usual bear-hug.

Strangely, Randy did not seem pleased. A little pout appeared on his face, suddenly serious. "Dad! Don't you remember your promise?"

Durk fell back, appalled. "Promise, son?"

"That we would shake hands, now that I've grown up." Randy looked hurt. "And now you treat me like a *child* again. Oh, Dad."

Randy ran out of the room. Durk was still unhappier when he saw Ellen's eyes on him, sharp, inquisitive. And uncertain. But she smiled and said, "I know how the worries of your lab work can make you forget things." But she didn't sound convincing.

Durk began to wish he had never come. Never tried to steal this golden hour in place of his double. He was in trouble. Could he fake it out for the rest of the time?

Wendy came dancing up. "Read me my favorite new book, Daddy," she pleaded. "I know it isn't bedtime but I can't wait to hear it again. Please, sugar please?"

"Favorite book," faltered Durk, feeling the pit yawning.

"Up there on the book shelf," sang Wendy. "I can't reach it. Get it down, Daddy."

Durk stood up and turned to the bookshelves that lined one wall. He could see the stack of children's picture books for five-year-olds easily enough. But which one was her favorite? His eyes swam as he looked over the titles on the spine.

Little Black Sambo... The Merry Tugboat... My First Party... The Wicked Wizard... The Picnic Adventure. Some of the titles Durk remembered—Wendy held onto things tenaciously—but the others were all new, bought in the past year. Bought, no doubt, by the other Durk.

Durk had to take a chance, especially since he knew that Ellen was watching him with an intent, wondering stare at his hesitation. With a silent prayer on his lips, Durk closed his eyes and pulled out a book. It was titled *The Prettiest Princess.*

"Oh, Daddy!" came from Wendy, her little face screwed up in disappointment. "*My favorite is Farm Animal Frolics.* Daddy, you don't care about me anymore…"

Wendy ran from the room in a storm of sudden tears. Durk knew his face was ashen. Ellen came slowly toward him, her sapphire eyes staring as if looking him through and through. "Dear, either you're overworking and need a doctor or—" She went on with remorseless intensity. "Or, you're not Wayne Durk, my husband. You're acting peculiarly, in many tiny ways. Well?"

Somehow, Durk managed to smooth it over with a flow of doubletalk that seemed to mollify Ellen's suspicions. He made a quick peace with the kids and then left, striding away rapidly. But that evening, when his double came home, Durk was lurking at the livingroom window outside and heard.

"Dear," said Ellen. "You acted so queerly when you came home today for a while."

"Came home?" sounded the surprised voice of the Durk recreate. "Ellen, are you imagining things? I haven't left the lab all day."

Shocked silence, followed by Ellen's horrified hiss. *"Then who was that man masquerading as you, my husband?"*

CHAPTER 7

Durk sat bolt upright, with clammy sweat running down his cheeks. His daydream was over. And now he saw in vivid starkness how impossible it was for him even to steal one hour at home. Or one second.

The inexorable blasting result would be the other Durk aware of having a "double," and of Ellen beginning a nightmare life in which all her security had been smashed. Doubts and fearful speculations would engulf her every time she saw the other Durk. Her life would be robbed of all serenity, from that day forward, wondering and waiting for a lurking impostor to show up again, one so nearly like her husband that it was uncanny, monstrous, soul-shattering.

And *his* life—the recreate's would also be volcanically blown up. Durk had to think of that, too. He could not ignore the devastating psychological upheaval that the Durk double would have to face. He would have to bid goodbye to the woman he had lived with and loved for a year—and all his lifetime, in his memories. He would have to kiss Wendy and hug—no, shake hands with Randy—for the last time. Then he would have to walk out and never turn back… and go on to what kind of broken life?

And Ellen, in full knowledge of what had happened, would be forced to welcome back the man she had last seen a year ago, and pretend that it was all the same.

All the same? *Nothing would be the same, for any of them.* Three people, and two children, would be living a mockery, a travesty, actors in some hideous play written by a fiend.

Durk sighed thankfully that it had only been a daydream. By letting it take him over in all its could-be detail, he knew now the fearful pit that lay before him if he really tried it. It was sheer madness, doomed to failure. Instead of an hour of happiness re-won, it would be an hour of disaster followed by lifelong purgatory.

Durk set his lips together tightly. That was that. Poignant words reverberated in his mind—*Farewell! Farewell forever to my former life… to Ellen… to Randy… to Wendy.* They now belonged to another man, and Durk had no right to wrest them back. In the gamble of life, he had lost all.

And now, what did he face? Besides a lonely life hagridden with memories, he had to battle the Bug. And try to save a crumbling world earmarked for doom. Durk glanced out of the window up in the night sky.

Why hadn't he died up there? Why had he survived, against all fantastic odds, to be catapulted back to earth? A dying civilization. A wrecked life. Those were his rewards.

Pick up the pieces and start again. But where are the pieces?

* * * *

"Good day, Dr. Durk," said the visitor, holding out a metallic ID card that was stamped—DR. CECIL G. WRIGHT, BIONICS.

The chief of the virology lab looked him over. Tall and spare like himself but with a brush mustache and close-cropped hair. The color of his eyes could not be seen behind dark glasses.

"You probably haven't heard of me," said the visitor in a polished manner, bowing slightly. "I'm an American but have worked in the Anzac Province for many years. The Bug mostly, for a decade. Looking for a bionic angle to its pathology. Without success, I'm afraid."

"You and me both, Dr. Wright," sighed "Durk," waving around his lab.

Durk, in his simple disguise—or guise—breathed easier. His first confrontation with his double had aroused no suspicions whatsoever. With Ellen it would be different but there would be no necessity to face her. He only had to establish himself in the workaday world as a visiting scientist from across the world, with an important new post.

Running the Recreate Lab wouldn't necessarily bring Durk and his double together. But Durk had been afraid of suddenly bumping into his recreate, somewhere in the city at an odd moment. The unexpected encounter might, at first glance, give the Durk-double a shock at the similarity between himself and "Wright." Better that Durk deliberately meet him and take the curse off. His assumed scientific status once established, it would then camouflage Durk completely, to a scientific mind like the double's. And one danger would be eliminated, of the recreate "Durk" ever knowing he was a recreate.

Durk-Wright now took his first searching look at the other Durk. Was he really his double down to the last atom? No... wait. There was something out of place. Something different... ah. His hair was parted on the *left* side. And a barely visible mole under his chin was on the *right* side of his face, again the *wrong* side. He was Durk turned wrongside to and a faint exultation rose within Durk.

Unconsciously, his hand went to the mole on his own chin. He started. It was on the *right* side. And with a moment's thought he knew that his own hair was parted on the *left* also. A shock went through Durk, as the truth struck him like a blow.

There was nothing "wrong" with the Durk double at all. He looked strange simply because he was *not a mirror image*. A man was so used to seeing his face in a mirror, day after day, that his reversed image seemed the right one. Seeing his own face as others saw it therefore seemed "wrong". And with a sinking heart, Durk knew now that they were literally and completely *identical* twins, the most perfect pair on earth. Durk's last hope, that his double was somehow imperfect, had been snatched away, leaving him hollow inside. He cut off his tormenting thoughts, realizing his double's lips were moving.

"Anything I can do for you?" the double was saying politely. "Data on our BV-IQ work is open for you."

"No, no," said Durk-Wright quickly. "As a matter of fact, I won't be doing Bug research now. You see, I've been appointed to a post in the BWB, under Finnegan Lloyd."

"Then we're under the same chief," said Durk's double, smiling in a sort of camaraderie. "What's your field of work?"

"The usual. Distribution of scientific brainpower around the world." Durk could not tell his true post as the Recreate Lab was top secret to all but those on a "need to know" basis. He went on, "I came merely to inquire whether you feel you need more help here. This is important work. You're the world's top virologist with no equal."

Durk laughed silently and mirthlessly within himself. No equal except himself. And they both had the greatest IQ on earth.

"Thanks," Durk said—the double was now *Durk* in his mind, an identity that he himself could never win back. And he might as well think of himself as *Wright* all the time and get used to it. Why play tormenting games with himself?

"As for help," said Durk, pursing his lips and looking around at the lab, "yes, if possible. As you perhaps know, if you've been briefed, two of my best men were lost in the past year—to the Brain Bug, of course..." Durk looked strained for a moment. Wright knew what was flashing through his mind—*why haven't I been stricken with my high IQ?* It was a worrisome thought that lurked in the minds of both Durks... Wright shuddered slightly and answered Durk.

"Hmm, two men of the caliber of Pulsudski and Vorranno—I've been briefed about your lab, you see—are going to be hard to find. You understand... the world shortage..."

"Quite."

"But I think I can give you one replacement anyway." Wright-Durk felt a wry twinge at the world "replacement." Actually, that was what Durk would get—a recreate, a literal replacement.

"That will help," nodded Durk, tiredly. "I should mention honestly that our lab hasn't achieved anything in the way of the Bug's pathology. Not one whit. It's still as much of a mystery as eleven years ago…"

"No need to apologize," put in Wright quickly. "The point is that your lab is the best *hope* of a Bug breakthrough, to call it that. Tomorrow you might stumble on the big clue that leads to understanding how the Bug epidemic spreads and is transmitted from victim to victim."

Tomorrow. How many times had Durk-Wright told that to himself in the past years, trying to rally himself out of hair-tearing discouragement. He felt a momentary twinge of jealousy at the thought that if the breakthrough came, it would be his double who had achieved it and would gain the honors. Or would he feel a vicarious pride, knowing that his own brain—though duplicated as a separate entity—had done it? Wright-Durk decided to wait for that time, if it ever came, before he could predict his reaction. Having the perfect "twin" brought up a whole new set of psychological ramifications that was unknown to psychiatry.

"Hope you're right," Durk was saying, with more fervor than his light words indicated.

Durk-Wright turned to go, with a last glance and sigh at the busy people in the lab. People he knew intimately but whom he could not greet as in the old days. To them he was a total stranger from another province of the Terran World Union.

"You'll hear from me soon," he promised, striding out. He leaned against the wall outside for a moment, collecting himself. It had been more of a nervous strain than he first thought. Meeting your double face to face, your carbon-copy peer, was a soul-twisting experience. Durk-Wright would report it to the psychiatric team at Recreate Labs. They needed every bit of psy-data they could get, in order to handle the emotional storms of new recreates—and their originals.

Durk-Wright stepped away from the lab, knowing it could never be his again. His old life had ended with the finality of a door slamming shut.

The door had opened to his new life. *So long, Wayne Durk… and I mean myself. So long, forever…*

* * * *

At the Oceanic Reclamation Plant floating on its giant pontoons in the South Atlantic, the vats began to bubble over with a purplish scum. The technician on duty hastily shut off the feed valves and called the manager.

The manager stooped to dab his finger in the purple goo, some of which had spilled on the floor, and tasted it carefully. He made a sour face. "Bad. Spoiled. Probably poisoned. Call the nutrition chemist for an analysis..." He stopped in consternation. "Oh, my God. I forgot. Dr. Tyrone died last week."

"And without him, or another chemist, we can't find out what's gone wrong with this batch." The technician turned and pointed in horror at another giant vat. "Look. That proteinizer's gone bad too."

The manager stood helplessly. No one else, in their entire working staff of twenty-eight, could possibly trace the cause of this disaster back to its origin, step by chemical step. From raw plankton gathered in the ocean by huge suction pipes, to the final diversified products—grey flour, nutritious proteins without fish-flavor, potato-like mash, and a crinkly breakfast food—involved a complex series of chemical manipulations whose intricacies were only known to a highly trained scientific mind.

That man was gone. The BWB, when contacted a week ago after Tyrone's death, had promised to rush a replacement for the chemist—in a *month*. In that time, 50,000 tons of plankton products would spoil in the vats and never reach the market.

Several hundred thousand people would miss meals, adding to the growing ranks of those with malnutrition. Ever since 1978, when the population explosion had forced mankind to "farm" the oceans for its unexploited calories, plankton processing had become a major source of food for the world. Each plankton plant that suffered a decline in production, or went out of operation, was a blow to the stomachs of hungry humanity.

CHAPTER 8

"Plankton Plant #83 on red call," said Finnegan Lloyd, shuffling the daily reports. "Batches turning out bad. Something wrong in the chemical system. Their chemist died a week ago."

"From Brain Rot?" asked Wright, unnecessarily. The Dr. Wright who had once—it seemed so long ago—been Dr. Durk.

"What else?" muttered Lloyd. "They need a new chemist pronto. Can do?"

Durk ran his eye up and down a list of scientists who had been called in for the recreate program. "Yes, here's one who qualifies. Dr. Stulnic of Yugoslavia. I'll rush him through the taper and you can get his double down there by tomorrow."

He snapped on the intercom and gave the instructions. Then he leaned back, rubbing his cheek wearily. He stared hollowly at Lloyd. "That's one gap we plugged but we missed a dozen others yesterday. We've got to keep stepping up our recreate rate. It's only 500 per day now."

"*Only* 500?" echoed Lloyd, somewhat surprised. He had not that closely followed the Recreate Lab's progress under Wright in the past three months. "And that isn't enough?"

Durk looked cynical. "You never put the thing on a worldwide all-inclusive basis before. Here are the cold, hard figures. It's not only the replacement of scientists who are involved but all people over IQ 125 who are in non-scientific fields. A few must be weeded out. People with IQ 125 are found working as truck drivers, doormen, and beauticians too. They are not all necessarily in key jobs."

"Wonder how that happens?" mused Lloyd, irrelevantly.

Durk shrugged. "Lack of ambition. Too many kicks in the face in early years. Or perhaps a plain matter of choice. A man with IQ 125 or over can do a low-intelligence job for living expenses and spend his leisure time in high-intelligence hobbies or avocations. Which might, for all we know, be the smart thing to do…"

They looked guiltily at each other, both at the moment wistful at the thought. Durk shook his head wryly.

"At any rate, most people over IQ 125 are in responsible jobs and are irreplaceable by lower IQ persons. Executives, decision-makers, planners, and such, in all areas of human life. They are the ones dying off from the Brain Bug, as well as scientists. Now to give you the rough totals I've gathered…"

Durk took a deep breath and read from a paper.

"Out of 6 billion people on earth today in 1998, approximately 100 million are of IQ 125 and up. All those over 155 are gone, victims of the Brain Bug."

They both shuddered at the stark reality of it. *Intellectotide*, thought Wright-Durk, on a par with genocide. And one tiny creature was doing it, not even as big as a one-celled animal. A mere viral molecule, on the borderline between inorganic and organic life.

He rustled the paper and went on, his throat already dry.

"Of the 100 million high-IQ people left, 10 million are scientists. But we have to deal with the larger group. In essence they are the brains and leadership of the world."

"Without them," Lloyd put in, "civilization is like a chicken—cliché or not—with its head cut off."

Durk went on. "The death rate among the 100 million 'brains' is one percent per year or *2150 per day*. Yes, a staggering figure. It's twice the normal death rate. That's how bad the Brain Bug epidemic is."

Lloyd was looking stunned as if struck by a heavy blow. "You mean we have to gear up to 2750 life-tapes and recreates per day?"

"Five times our present rate and more," nodded Durk. "The question is, how soon can you expand our facilities to reach this rate?"

"Well, as far as room goes," said Lloyd, unworriedly, "no sweat. Earthia City, as you know, was built over the semi-ruins of the former New York City after it became one vast slum and ceased to function as a metropolis. Because of the intense nuclear war threat of 1985, an enormous bomb shelter was hollowed out underneath Erthia City, a deep down in the bedrock of Manhattan Island. The bomb shelter fell into disuse when the formation of the Terran World Union in 1988 eliminated all further threat of atomic war. Recreate Labs at present only occupies a piddling part of the giant cavern meant to house a million people at least. So we can expand our facilities without lack of room."

Lloyd now groaned unhappily. "But it's the equipment and personnel that are the headache. And the cost. Don't forget I have to talk the TWITs Brain Commission into it. And Josas de Milleaux, in turn, has to pry the funds from the government budget. This will call for billions and billions…"

Durk spoke quietly. "Is it too much to pay for saving civilization?"

"I know, I know. There's no argument. But the TVVU is always yammering for science to lick the Bug itself. Wipe it out, then no more trouble." He looked at Durk intently. "Tell me, Durk... I mean, Wright... I shouldn't blunder like that... tell me, is there any chance of achieving the shortcut and finding a way of stopping the Brain Bug itself? After eleven years of frantic research around the world, by the best virologists, pathologists, biochemists and all, nothing has happened. What does it mean?"

Wright got to his feet, thinking Durk thoughts of the old days. "It means we've got a virus that strikes suddenly, in a man's brain, if it's IQ 125 or over. The disease is contagious but there is no known method of transmission from victim to victim. The virus cannot be halted in its ravages, by any known drug or treatment. It means, in medical terms, something impossible, weird, uncanny..."

His teeth were grinding, as they often had during his researches on the Bug. "Yet there has to be an answer. No form of life, or pseudo-life such as a virus, can be immune to *some* form of destruction. The Black Plague killed off one-third of the human race in the Middle Ages, but it was finally licked. Maybe not by medical science but by the human body's ability to build up resistance, to form anti-bodies. A good part of the Brain Bug research has been to find such anti-bodies. Computers are running through every possible chemical known or hitherto unknown. Thousands came up as faint possibilities. But when they were tried in a culture of the Brain Bug, the Bug won out."

"Cultures of the Brain Bug in your lab," shivered Lloyd. "You used vacuum-seal remote-control methods, of course. If any culture broke loose..."

"One did." Durk suddenly stopped pacing, surprised wonder in his face. "The seal broke, about 5 years ago. The culture was actually sprayed through the air. We must have all breathed in the virus, unavoidably. Yet not one of us—all high IQ people—was stricken by the disease." He pounded a helpless fist into his other palm. "That only adds to the damnable riddle. It means the disease does not traditionally attack through the bloodstream. Then how *does* it happen?"

A faraway look came into his tortured eyes.

"I think, Lloyd... I think we're up against a mystery beyond the grasp of orthodox science. Beyond the frontier of medical knowledge. A new form of life, viral life, that may inherit the earth in time..."

"You don't think we can lick it?" Lloyd whispered.

"Do you?"

"But that only means the death of all extra-intelligent people," said Lloyd almost calmly. "Including you and me. It won't touch the rest of humanity, by far the larger part. Earth will still have a population of close to six billions…"

"In a broken-down society that can't support half that number," Durk hissed. "With the top brainpower gone, and nobody to run the machines and labs, civilization will fall into ruin. The culture will return to non-technological savagery. Mankind will be thrown back a thousand years or more."

"Well, at least," said Lloyd almost cheerfully, "the Brain Bug will die out too if it can only feed on high-IQ brains." His voice became more vibrant, approaching his usual forcefulness. "But our program can still work out. The recreate process is the god-send. By re-staffing the world with duplicated high-powered brains, we can stave off the worst and give the medicos time to solve the Brain Bug riddle." He faced Durk with more of his normal bulldog air. "You'll get the expanded Recreate Labs, I promise you, if Milleaux and I have to raid the treasury ourselves."

Durk smiled his thanks. "By the way, Lloyd, you have an appointment down in my place this afternoon."

"For what?" Lloyd was puzzled.

"A life-tape."

"Huh?"

"We can't risk losing your recreate, when you have an IQ of 148. Be sure to show up."

And just be sure, Wright-Durk's thoughts went on bitterly, that your recreate doesn't take your place at the office, and at home…

* * * *

Durk stepped into the psychiatrist's office. Doctor J. P. Gordon looked harried. He whispered in Durk's ear, pointing to a dark-skinned man sitting slumped in an easy chair.

"This recreate of Dr. Abdul Shekka is in a state of defiance. Refuses to carry on."

"Does he know—"

"Oh, yes. He quickly accepted the fact that he was a recreate. But the revelation induced a shock trauma in his sensitive mind. He won't listen to reason. He demands to be exterminated. Sorry to call you here, sir, but I thought you might talk to him. Being the man with the first recreate, you might impress him."

Durk sat down opposite the sullen-faced recreate. "I'm Dr. Cecil Wright, chief of this place. My recreate was the first one made and he is doing well."

No answer.

"You are alive, as alive as I am. Or your original. You can live just as we do, with full rights and privileges. That was a law enforced immediately in Recreate Lab's rules. There is no discrimination against you. You are not looked upon as a freak. You are respected as fully as any other human being. For you *are* a human being."

A gleam flashed in Dr. Shekka's eyes, a fanatic gleam.

"No, I am not a human being. Allah did not mean for human mockeries to be created in laboratories."

So that was it, thought Durk. Religious scruples despite his scientific training. Heresy, blasphemy, unsanctioned by the Koran. What line of attack to use?

"When a son is born, who is the creator, here on earth?"

"Why, the father," said Dr. Shekka. "But please, Dr. Wright, do not try any emotional or philosophical tricks with me. Don't insult my intelligence—my borrowed intelligence."

"But let me pursue that other thought," insisted Durk. "Every person born on earth comes out of the genetic coding of his father. From his father's genetic 'tape', we might say."

"Semantics," snorted the recreate. "That is the natural, the Allah-given, process. This," he waved around vaguely, "is a man having a life-tape for a mother."

Durk had to ponder that for a moment. A new twist to this mind-numbing problem. The original Dr. Shekka no doubt was devoted to his parents and family, as Arabians usually were. The blasting thought must have hit the recreate that he could never return to his home. They had never had "twins." And his "mother" was not really his mother. A life-tape was.

Durk's thoughts whirled, seeking a better approach. "Does Dr. Shekka—the other one—*own* his brain and body if it came from Allah?"

"Why… uh…" The recreate's eyes shifted, thinking deeply. "In the religious sense, no. All of us are Children of Allah—or of God to use the Christian term."

"If that is so," Durk bored in, seeing a chink in his armor, "why cannot Allah allow that same body-brain to be born again, in a different way?"

"But Allah did not do it," protested the recreate.

"How do *you* know?" demanded Durk. "How do you know but that Allah himself intervened in this hour of peril for his children on earth? Since he could not change the age-old system of sexual reproduction or speed it up, why would he not then allow or inspire us to achieve the tape-regeneration method? In a way, it's just another form of reincarnation."

Durk could see he had hit home, for many Orientals and near-east people believed in reincarnation.

"Do you believe that through Allah comes all our ideas and inspirations?" Durk bored on.

"Of course, in the final analysis, since he created us…"

Durk drove on quickly. "Then the concept of the life-tape must be part of Allah's great plan, in this crisis facing the human race. Surely he cannot stand by and see us wiped out brutally, by a tiny virus." Durk changed his tone. "As a man of science, do you think all the great advances of science are unblessed by Allah?"

"I… uh… no. Certainly Allah must see that what science has done is good, in the main. But this…"

"Is it a bad thing, like the nuclear bomb? Will it harm humanity? Or is it a battle, a good fight, against extinction? And again I must ask, how do *you* of your own knowledge, know that Allah does *not* sanction man-made recreates which can save his children on earth?"

Dr. Shekka stared back dumbly, lips working.

"Do you not accept the possibility that Allah, who works in devious ways, himself inspired the life-tape concept among us? And in that case, Allah is your father even if your life-tape is your 'mother.'"

A sudden smile broke over Dr. Shekka's face. "As a man who is deeply religious, Dr. Wright, I must admit you have given me a new outlook. Or let us say, to put it another way, that you have nicely confused the issue to the point where I have no further clear-cut objections to being a recreated man. I suppose I might as well take the philosophical viewpoint that since I am, I am. As a duplicated man of science, I will be glad to utilize the gift of my mind and not waste it."

"And as a *man* in his own right," said Durk heartily, "let me shake your hand."

There was a glow in Dr. Shekka's eyes as he solemnly took Durk's extended hand.

The psychiatrist looked astounded. He whispered to Durk as he left, "What a headshrinker you would have been!"

Durk felt his mind and spirit shrinking as he walked away. No doubt the Shekka recreate wished he were the original man. Conversely, Wright wished he were his recreate, so he could go home to Ellen and the kids. Perhaps this recreate project *was* an evil thing…

Durk had to shake that foreboding thought out of his mind.

CHAPTER 9

She worked in the recreate department that handled life-tape recordings. Her name was Lenora Colfax. She had sapphire blue eyes and a pert nose. She walked with easy grace and her voice was lilting. She had blond hair neatly coiffured and smiled in a heartwarming way. She was so much like Ellen that Wright-Durk started when he first saw her.

For a moment he thought, wildly, that she was a recreate of his wife. Had Finnegan Lloyd insanely created Ellen's double, in some twisted belief that she could console Durk as a substitute wife? But as Durk shook his head to clear his vision, his nerves eased.

Face too long, eyebrows arched quite differently, a dimple in both cheeks... no, she was only the usual kind of accidental "double". An old-time movie disclaimer filtered into his mind in paraphrased form—any resemblance between Lenora Colfax and Ellen Durk was purely coincidental. Yet that resemblance was close enough to make the girl, through squinted eyes, look almost exactly like Ellen.

And thereby began a fantastic new struggle for Durk. He tried to ignore her, dismiss her from his thoughts, but it didn't work. One day he impulsively asked her to lunch. She looked a bit surprised but accepted without hesitation.

First he thought of taking her to a small out-of-way restaurant so as not to attract attention. But then he suddenly laughed at himself, morosely. He wasn't a married man secretly striking up an affair with another woman. As Cecil Wright, he was a free man, a bachelor. At this bitter point in his thoughts, he laughed again, and took her to an ostentatious place in the neighborhood. It simply did not matter if he was seen with her. There would be no gossip, except perhaps about the "chief" for the first time showing any romantic leanings.

When they were seated at a table, Lenora said frankly, "I'm flattered that you pay attention to me. You're practically God around the labs, you know."

"God?" He laughed. "You mean because I'm the head man?"

"Yes. But I mean it in another way," she said rather solemnly. "After all, you are creating human beings, just as God did Adam and all who followed."

Durk pondered that, astounded. He had never thought of it that way. But he saw the twinkle in her eyes. "I may be God but I have a human appetite. Let's order."

She grinned and he felt perfectly at ease with her. They talked shop for a while, and a growing feeling of intimacy rose in Durk. During the course of the conversation, it came out that she was not only unmarried but had no serious attachments, by her own admission.

Durk felt his heart leap. If he were to marry again, this kind of girl would be his choice. *Marry again?* The thought turmoiled into his mind, shockingly. But he was already married—*or was he?* Ellen lived with the other Durk as husband and wife. That left Durk himself free, legally and morally. The devastating impact of this unique situation left him almost gasping. He could marry again.

"Is something wrong?" Lenora asked, peering at his blood-drained face anxiously.

"No, no." He grinned weakly, and pretended to dive into his food hungrily, though his appetite had vanished.

She abruptly changed the subject. "You know, I'd hate to be a recreate if I were a man. Just think of them having to give up—in their thoughts—their lives with a wife and children. They suddenly realize they have no family and would have to marry again if they wanted one."

Durk almost dropped his fork. What would she say if she knew *his* situation, which was reversed? And thereby much more of a tormenting dilemma. A recreate had not really lost a family, except in his memories. Durk had suffered the real thing, the ultimate penalty.

"Damn blast the recreate program!" he blurted out, in his inner agony.

She stared at him levelly. "A rather strange thing for the head of the program to say."

Durk was aghast at himself. "I... uh... meant..."

"I understand," she said quickly. "You mean all the problems it brings up and all the human feelings that have to be trampled upon. Yet it's necessary, isn't it, to fight the Brain Bug."

"Naturally," said Durk, glad that she had unwittingly covered up for him. He looked into the girl's cerulean eyes, so like those of Ellen. Would he, and should he, think of marrying again?

Then another thought stole into his mind. *What if the other Durk died from the Brain Blight?* Then perhaps, if it were kept secret from Ellen, he could slip into the double's place and resume his former life. He almost panted at the thought.

But again, this led to another searing thought. So far, no recreate had been stricken with the Brian Bug. Of course, their numbers were still small, a few thousand compared to the millions of living scientists. But were the recreates somehow *immune?* Did some subtle factor in the electronic recreation of a brain make it resistant to the Bug?

If so, it would be hopeless for Durk to await his double's possible death. Not that he would wish it but only taking in the possibilities. And that again left him nowhere in his personal life.

Before he could marry again, he would have to wait it out and see if the recreates were really immune. If they were, Durk would face the loss of Ellen for life and would have to think of marrying again—and feel like a bigamist, though clear by all laws and moral codes.

If they were not immune, then Durk would face an uncertain wait for years, perhaps a lifetime, without any assurance which way fate would turn. Maddening… Exquisite torture…

Durk schooled himself so that his tormenting thoughts did not reflect in his face and alarm the girl. "Let's have dinner together some time," he invited, as they were ready to leave. She agreed and Durk felt guilty. He would be holding her on a string, a puppet in the private play of his life, which could turn either way, for her or against her.

Durk forced himself to make light remarks during the airtaxi trip back to the BWB. Then they took the guarded elevators down to the immense underground establishment that the world at large was yet unaware of.

The place where a Godlike machine, if not a God, was creating living men out of the whole cloth of manufactured matter molded into human flesh and blood. And into human minds and emotions.

* * * *

During the next monthly summary session between Durk and Lloyd, regarding the Recreate Labs program, Durk brought up a routine matter.

"I've tightened up the screening of the scientific group. Just as some high-IQ people hold ordinary jobs and are not of use in our program to refill the world brainbank, so certain scientists must be left out. Take an archeologist who all his life has dug up ancient artifacts relating to mankind's past history. Or an anthropologist who unearths old fossils and adds another piece to the evolutionary jigsaw puzzle. They are not really of importance to the world, taking the strictly materialistic viewpoint. At least, not vital to world *survival.*"

Lloyd nodded. "That makes sense. We need the doers, the designers, the decision-makers in vital areas of human life today."

"Still, we modified the screening to include any such cultural scientists—to call them that—in case they were willing to give up their former careers. An archeologist, for instance, can be trained to supervise a manufacturing plant producing modem artifacts—tools, or dry goods, or dishware. Those that are willing will then have life-tapes made, but *after* their training into the new job, so that the recreate will inherit the training."

"Free training, so to speak," said Lloyd whimsically. "Why pay twice for the course?"

Durk now got to what was gnawing in his mind.

"The first thing I did as chief of Recreate Labs, as you know, was to have life-tapes made of the recreates too, as fast as they were produced. That was a precaution in case both the original man and his recreate died. In some cases, with the brainpower shortage around the world, they are indispensable men of specialized talents that we would lose forever."

"We couldn't afford to," agreed Lloyd. "It was a very brilliant innovation."

"But is it useless? A waste of effort?" said Durk, puffing slowly at his *Grande* cigar.

"Are you serious?" Lloyd was astonished. "It's insurance. Protection in depth in case the recreate of a dead scientist also dies from the Brain Rot."

"But what if the recreates are immune?"

Lloyd started. "Immune? But—"

"Look," snapped Durk. "Maybe it's too soon to tell but the record shows that not one of our recreates—some 100,000 to date—has contracted the BV-IQ disease."

"But their total is less than one-thousandth of the total number of living people over IQ 125."

"But the death rate is 1% per year for those people," said Durk incisively. "Even in three months that means 250,000 dead. By odds of two-and-one-half to one there should have been recreate deaths before this."

Lloyd jumped up excitedly. "You're right, Durk," he said with an uplift in his voice. "If true, that means we've got the battle won, even if we have to recreate every scientist on earth. The originals may die off from the Bug but the recreates will live on. The epidemic will be over. Man, what a stroke of luck!"

Durk's fixed smile was meant to share Lloyd's enthusiasm. But within himself he felt as if he had died. The seeming survival factor of the recreates meant his own "death"—as Wayne Durk. For then his double would live on and on, defying the Brain Bug.

Irony again. Exquisite irony that only a mocking fate could have devised. If the doubles were immune, earth won out—but Durk lost. The other way around was hardly better. Durk might win if his double died—but earth might die too.

Wildly, unable to bear this kind of mental whiplashing, Durk changed the topic, fumbling at his papers.

"A new problem is shaping up. Out of the originals of the 100,000 recreates we've made, some 250 died in these last three months. The latest is Dr. Swenson, nuclear scientist of Sweden. He died of Brain Rot, leaving his recreate alive alone, and now working at another important post, while another recreate took over Swenson's job."

"What about it?" drawled Lloyd, unexcited. "The beauty of our recreate program is that the minute a key man gets caught by the Bug some recreate fills his shoes without an effort."

"Yes, but what about Swenson's *family*?" said Durk broodingly. "He has a wife and seven children."

"Oh, boy," groaned Lloyd. "Another king-sized headache."

"Bigger than you think," responded Durk gloomily. "What have you been doing in the 250 cases that already have happened?"

"Nothing, really," confessed Lloyd, mopping his bald head. "We've briefed the recreate into his new job without telling the family about it. He doesn't go home to them. Too awkward to bridge the gap and get them together."

"Heartless," snapped Durk. "A man does not live by work alone—nor a recreate. The other half of his life at home should be restored, if possible."

Lloyd was thinking. "Maybe we can have the psychiatric staff work on it and dream up some way to have the recreate… uh… reintroduced to his family. If we explain how he is the exact *reincarnation* of the dead man…"

"Would you like to try?" hissed Durk.

"I'd rather fight a dragon," admitted Lloyd, his fat frame quivering.

"But that calls for another policy change in our program," Durk went on, practically. "When Swenson was stricken, his family was immediately notified. But hereafter, we'll make it a strict order that at the first sign of the Brain Blight, the victim is to be isolated in a hospital, unknown to his family. Since death is 100% inevitable, his recreate is to take over his job and his home life immediately. There will be no interruption in his home affairs. The wife and children will suspect nothing."

"No?" challenged Lloyd. "What about the memories of home life the recreate does *not* have? Memories of the period while the original man still lived at home. Remember that the recreates are being brought to life *before* the original's death, which may be months later. You can't plant those missing home memories in a recreate. He'll show up as a phony to a wife."

"Not if we carefully concoct a story that a lab accident gave the man amnesia." Durk was feeling his way, in this new and untried wilderness of human reactions that came out of the existence of double men. It was all a groping, and improvising, a patch-up job. But what else was there to do? Whatever could be salvaged in human relationships to prevent tragic heartbreak had to be done, no matter what distasteful tricks were required.

"*Something* can be cooked up to cover that lack of memory," he went on firmly. "Then the recreate can move in with the family and take up the former man's role, without difficulty. Best of all, he will have all the drive and incentive necessary, too. In his mind, he has lived with them all his life and loves them, just as the man who died did. In fact, any recreate should be deliriously happy—assuming there was a good home life—that it happened. He will wonder how lucky he can be."

Durk knew that for sure, for it was only the reverse of his own situation. Certainly he would be deliriously overjoyed if his double died and he, Durk, could return to the warmth of his home. Only in his case there was a formidable barrier—if recreates were immune.

"Okay," Lloyd was saying, thoughtfully. "We'll institute your plan right away. That will take care of further cases when the original man dies and his own recreate is promoted into his spot. But we can't do anything about poor Mrs. Swenson…"

"I'm going to try, by God," exploded Durk, banging his fist on the desk. "I'm going to fly there myself and see if I can reconcile her to accepting the recreate of her husband in his place, for the children's sake if nothing else. Kids will accept if the mother will, being more adaptable."

Would he be trying the impossible? Durk didn't know. Nobody knew. The case had never come up before in all human history. In a sense, he realized, he was a pioneer into a vast new domain of human relationships, uncharted and unexplored. He had to discover, if he could, a new world where recreated doubles of men were accepted without discrimination in the arena of love between a man and a woman. And between a recreate and a woman…

CHAPTER 10

Mrs. August Swenson was dry-eyed, sitting in proud dignity. She had sent the children out to play or do chores around their semi-country place. Her first few words of greeting encouraged Durk, indicating a well-balanced mind of good caliber. She obviously did not let emotions overrule her or run away with her. A good test case, in the event more would occur by chance where the wife heard of her husband's death despite attempts at concealment.

"I cannot tell you just who I am or what establishment I run," Durk said, carefully, with Recreate Labs still under strict security. "But it is a very important project with full backing of the TWU government."

She was eyeing him keenly and was apparently satisfied that he was trustworthy, for she nodded and waited expectantly for his next words.

Durk had rehearsed some of it, but he knew he would have to improvise as he went along, on a grand scale. A frightening scale. With no guide lines to follow. None existed.

"Mrs. Swenson, do you believe in reincarnation?" he asked abruptly.

She looked startled. "Yes, and no. That is, I see nothing wrong with the concept, yet I do not think there is proof. I'm an agnostic."

Good enough. No preconceived prejudices, on that or anything else.

"But what if I told you that science has not only proved there is a form of reincarnation, but has actually achieved it?"

Mrs. Swenson was sharp enough to see where this might lead, and Durk could see the quickening light in her eyes and hear the catch in her breath. She was adding two and two, quite rapidly.

"I mean," Durk plunged on, hastening to the point sooner that he had planned, "that in our laboratories, we have *recreated* your dead husband. *Alive*."

First she stared at him indignantly, as if he were insulting her intelligence or mocking her. Then her expression became sheer disbelief. Finally, guarded curiosity shone from her eyes.

"My husband—recreated? I won't use the word impossible, since nothing really is. But how… *how?*"

Durk felt like cheering. She was open to hearing the process. In chosen words, but briefly, he gave the gist of the recreate program without violating security in essential details. Her eyes kept widening and she jerked as if little shocks were shaking her within the depths of her being. At the end she burst into tears.

Durk let her cry it out. Suddenly, she swept away the tears with a hanky, firmly and courageously. "I will have to accept what you say because, like my husband, you are a scientist who is only interested in seeking and telling the truth. But do you mean this... this recreated man is *exactly* like my husband?"

"Physically, mentally, emotionally, spiritually, down to the last atom and brain-cell and gland. Furthermore, he has every memory of your married life, except for a short period since he came alive. But this second Dr. Swenson is Dr. Swenson."

"I can't believe it," she murmured, overwhelmed and leaning back. "If it were true..."

She didn't finish. Durk quickly took it up. "I can arrange for you to meet him this afternoon. He has been told about this. And I want to tell you something, Mrs. Swenson—"

Durk paused and looked her in the eye, speaking slowly and emphatically. "When Dr. Swenson—the one now living—heard that with your consent, he might be accepted in your household as a father and husband, he broke down and cried too—in happiness. You see, in his mind and memories, he has really lived with you all your life. You are no stranger to him but a dearly beloved wife."

Mrs. Swenson's eyes seemed to plead for more. Durk was quite willing.

"He can remember the day, he told me, when he proposed to you out by the castle wall. The tender things he said. He told me of the happy yell he gave when your first child was born—he'll tell you the words he later whispered in your ear. Words that only you could know. He remembers the time he painted you and called it *Beauty*. And the time..."

"No—enough!" choked Mrs. Swenson. "It is tearing my heart apart. Please stop."

Durk was taken aback. Had he lost after all his eloquence, all his fierce desire to rectify a tragedy and bring new joy to a grieving heart?

But suddenly she sat up with a smile that was like dawn coming up over the hills. "Please bring him... Dr. Swenson... to me this afternoon."

When the recreate walked in later, the two of them stared at each other for a long moment. Then, as one, they rushed into each other's arms, murmuring endearments.

"Thank you, thank you, thank you," came drifting to Durk's ears, for he was already on his way out. He was no longer needed there. He had created something more than a double, he mused—he had this time created a patch of heaven for two people.

There were some rewards, after all, in this recreate program. Of course in some households—his thoughts turning practical—the recreate returning to the home would be the last thing a discontented or antagonistic wife would want, glad to be rid of her unwanted mate. Such was life.

* * * *

Wayne Durk, alias Cecil Wright, was glad he had to work hard at his job. It was the only anodyne for the hollow, empty feeling inside at the thought of losing Ellen and the children for life.

Three thousand men and women—the rate had been upped—called in each day, from around the world, to have their life-tapes made. It was an enormous logistics problem just to fly them back and forth. Durk's trained staff handled all the detail work, daily notifying the chosen group, picking them up, processing them through the life-tape procedure, then whisking them back to their jobs. All at a minimum loss of time, for all were high-IQ people in the key jobs that kept civilization limping along without stalling dead.

To handle this immense flow of brainpower in and out, the Recreate Labs were now a warren, a maze, a labyrinth that stretched for miles underground beneath Earthia City. Its staff ran into the thousands. The funds, steadily if not cheerfully, had been bestowed by the TWU budget bureau under the nagging of Josas de Milleaux of the Brain Blight Commission.

Finnegan Lloyd, in turn, had translated the money into the expanded facilities, added equipment, and swelling personnel. It was, in a sense, a Manhattan Project—oddly, under Manhattan itself—or an Apollo Moon Program, with a set goal, only on a still vaster scale. It was Custer's last stand against oblivion for the human race.

Durk winced whenever he saw a group of new men and women come in. They all had a hang-dog air, like condemned criminals. The life-taping only sharpened for them the axe under which these high-IQ people lived. Each knew that he could be the next victim of the Brain Rot, tomorrow. In fact, by the sheer weight of death-rate figures—the thought always smote Durk heavily—100,000 of the original high-IQ people would be gone, replaced by their recreates, within a year.

Still, Durk felt a solid satisfaction in the accomplishments of Recreate Labs. Facilities had been expanded under forced draft at 1998's speediest pace. At last, for the first time, they had caught up with and surpassed the death-rate among high-IQ people. No more plants, factories, or labs were being closed up for lack of brainpower. The recreates had plugged the gap.

Though tottering from the brain-killing epidemic in the past eleven years, civilization could now keep on its feet. And one golden promise lay ahead. By the random mixings of the genetic code, under the laws of heredity, the low-IQ people would again produce geniuses in another generation. If the Brain Rot had been conquered by then—it *must* be—the human race could again breed itself into braininess.

The recreates, Durk saw clearly, were the big white hope. They could keep filling the brainbank until the worst was over. And if they were truly immune to the Brain Bug, their numbers could in time be increased to slowly build up world brainpower to its former peak. True, it would be of lesser quality, shorn of pristine genius, but it would hold the fort until the next generation delivered its quota of towering minds.

Immunity to the Brain Bug. If Durk had a choice, would he like to have it? His mind forked into two paths over this. To live on without Ellen and the kids was like a sentence to lifelong torment. Yet to die before he was sure he could never regain them, via his double's death if it ever occurred…

Durk sighed and bent over his desk restlessly, getting back to the papers he had to sign. He never began, for the door was suddenly flung open and Finnegan Lloyd fairly leaped in, his fat jowls quivering.

"Durk! It happened!" he yelled hoarsely, waving three comsatograms. "Three recreates just came down with the Brain Rot."

Durk sagged. That would make their job doubly hard now, not only replacing the originals but filling in for the dying recreates as they came along. Perhaps their resistance had only been temporary and now the Bug was after them too.

Lloyd was eyeing Durk ominously, and the air seemed to be electrified. "And one of them is," Lloyd said in measured slowness, "—Dr. Wayne Durk."

"My recreate?" gasped Durk.

Lloyd nodded dumbly.

A giddy dream instantly flashed into Durk's mind—of being reunited with his family and regaining his former life. He felt no guilt over being glad that his double was stricken. After all, he was a lab-made creature, not a bona fide human. Then he felt ashamed of himself. But he gripped Lloyd's arm fiercely.

"Does Ellen know?"

"No, not yet."

"*Don't tell her*," barked Durk. "Say nothing. By tonight, when we have to account for his not coming home… well, things may take care of themselves. Come on, to the hospital."

"Wayne Durk" had been rushed to the special Brain Blight Hospital, which had no connection with BWB or Recreate Labs. Death had no part in the creation of new life. Durk-Wright stared down at the feverish form of his double, twisting and writhing in his bed. A team of nurses was frantically giving him intravenous injections, hypos of potent antibiotics, blood transfusions. Despite all previous failures, medical practice was dedicated to challenging death, hoping to stave it off against any odds.

They all knew it was hopeless. The fever-tortured victim would subside into a coma by the next day, then his brain would rot and wither away. What was buried with the body was an empty skull.

Durk trembled as he looked down at his double, entering the long death throes. In some flash of empathetic rapport, he could almost feel the searing head pains as the living brain was slowly invaded and destroyed. It was like looking at one's own death.

But along with that, something struggled to burst forth and sing in wild joy. Lloyd seemed to sense his thoughts and put a sympathetic hand on his shoulder. "If we work it right," he whispered softly, "you can secretly take his place, just as he took yours, and go home to your wife and children."

Durk turned in blazing fury. "You fool!" he snarled. "Is that why you think I came?" He wrenched off his coat and ripped off his shirt.

"Doctor," he bawled as one came in. "Live transfusion. Me to Dr. Wayne Durk. Then hook up a blood-machine and give me fresh blood as all mine is drained into the patient. Every drop of it. Understand?"

The doctor stared with mouth open. "You heard the, man," yelled Lloyd. As the doctor gave low orders to the nurses, Lloyd turned to Durk dumbfounded. "Why?"

"Because I may be the one who is immune," snapped Durk, wincing as the nurse inserted the needle-tube in his arm. "Just a blind, dirty hunch, that's all. Remember, I was frozen in space for a year and—who knows? And for my recreate to be stricken ahead of me… well, it adds up wrong. Crazy. So maybe it isn't so crazy to try this."

The ingenious blood-machine of 1998 fed artificial blood-plasma into Durk as his own veins poured their life-sustaining fluid into the fevered man. The two blood flows did not intermix in Durk's veins, diluting the product that went into his double. The artificial plasma Durk received was designed to be non-miscible with blood, to allow for entire draining of one man's blood into another man. When the transfusion was complete, fresh whole blood was pumped into Durk.

He felt no worse for the experience than a slight giddiness. The nurses gave him injections that perked him up.

"We've tried this time and time again," said the attendant doctor, somewhat sarcastically. "Replacing the patient's entire blood to the last drop didn't hinder the Brain Blight in the least—"

He broke off, staring at the patient. He had suddenly turned quiet and the flush began to fade away from his face. Astounded, the doctor took his temperature. He looked up, and his voice cracked. "The fever is broken! It means the disease was arrested." He stared at Durk, awed. "How could your blood do it, unless it carries anti-bodies against the Brain Rot?"

Putting on his shirt, Durk said tersely, "I'm sorry, Doctor. I can't tell you for security reasons."

The doctor spread his hands and shrugged.

Once they were out in the hall, Lloyd dragged Durk into a waiting room where no one sat except a little old man who seemed asleep. "Out with it, man," demanded Lloyd, still stunned by what had occurred. "You must have some inkling, some theory, as to your immunity."

Durk pondered and answered slowly. "My guess—and it's only a wild guess—is that during the year I was space-frozen, my errant spacecraft probably took a highly eccentric or elliptical orbit."

"Corroborated," nodded Lloyd. "We did retrieve your capsule from the top of that glacier, you know. The auto-tapes, which kept working for a while after your collision—probably with a meteoroid—recorded an apogee of 33,261 miles above earth."

Durk snapped his fingers. "Right up through the Van Allen Belt. That indicates strongly what I suspect—that the Van Allen radiations I absorbed, from daily baths for a year, gave me some kind of immunity to the Brain Bug."

A fever of excitement overtook Lloyd. "Then your space mission wasn't a failure after all. Not if you've brought back the golden key to lick the Bug." His face fell. "Of course, we can't ship ten million scientists up into the Van Allen Belt, plus all the recreates…"

"No, but we can analyze why or how the Van Allen radiations do the job. How they interact with the brain or the blood. Another space trip, and a lot of lab work on earth, and we may be able to duplicate the radiations down here. The anti-Bug radiations that would lick the epidemic."

Durk waved, tiredly. "But we'd better wait before we hire the brass band. My blood may have given my double only a temporary remission. We'll have to wait for further hospital reports before we're sure he's saved."

CHAPTER 11

Durk did not leave his office that night. He sat in the dark, staring out at the scattered city lights on an outside viewplate, waiting… waiting. When the optiphone rang, he leaped at it. The doctor's face on the screen was all one big beaming smile. "You told me to call you at any change, for the better or worse. I'm glad to make this report about the patient—pulse, normal…"

As the doctor read off a string of clinical terms, Durk interrupted harshly, "Cut the medical garbage, doctor. What does it all mean?"

"It means the patient is clearly out of danger, with all symptoms gone. Dr. Wayne Durk is the first man on earth to survive the Brain Blight. What this means to the world, sir—"

Rudely, Durk flipped the toggle and cut him off.

Yes, what it meant to the world was a new and wonderful chance to beat the Bug and keep civilization from staggering to its grave.

What it meant to Durk was the death of his last hope. By saving his double, he had cut his own throat. Barring death by accident or some ordinary disease—a comparatively rare chance in 1998—Durk's recreate would live to a ripe old age, perhaps even surviving Dr. Cecil Wright…

Durk cursed aloud and shook a fist at nothing in particular. The knife had been twisted in him over and over again. He cursed the day the recreate process had been developed. It had saved the world. But it had sent Durk's universe crashing around him.

In the dawn's pallid glow, he had worked all the frenzied rage out of his system. He was drained, empty, barely able to drag himself out for a bite to eat, before another busy day swept him up.

And he had to think. Think how to take advantage of this golden opportunity to lick the Bug. He hated the Bug most of all. It had first of all led to the recreate process which led to Durk's double which led to Durk's lifelong trap as Cecil Wright.

"I'll get that Brain Bug," Durk swore to himself with fanatic intensity, "so help me."

But something else bothered Durk. A series of small things that kept irritating him because they could not be pinned down or put in their proper place. They popped up when he took a grand view of the entire problem of the Brain Bug. Exasperated at the confusion as they milled around in his mind, he made a concerted effort now to sort them out and tick them off, one by one...

Despite vague theories about feeding on bio-currents, how could a virus systematically attack only high-horse-power brains? It almost seemed *deliberate*. How could it skip from brain to brain like a contagion, yet without any conceivable means of transmission? As if it were somehow directly *implanted* in the brain.

Where had the Brain Blight come from, since study proved it unrelated to any strains of viruses on earth before? Almost as if it were *brought* to earth.

Why had the recreates at first seemed immune, and then belatedly been struck? A blight would strike randomly. It was almost as if the Bug had been taken *unawares* by the recreates and turned its attention to them when realization dawned that victims presumably killed had suddenly been recreated. But that would almost mean *intelligent* surveillance of earthly brainpower.

And bolstering that thought, had the virus, when finding out Durk himself was immune, struck at his double? Logically, the original should be the first target... *if the plan was to systematically wipe out human brainpower.*

Conclusion? A damnable riddle that did not fit in solely or naturally with a pure viral disease. It had anomalies that fit another pattern—*deliberate planning.* Yet where did that lead to? Did that mean an *intelligent virus?*

Utterly fantastic, inconceivable. In fact, downright ridiculous. And yet... and yet...

Back in his office, Durk's involved ruminations were cut off as Finnegan Lloyd popped in, his fat face aglow.

"Just called the hospital. They're discharging Wayne Durk today."

"Good," said Durk, not knowing whether he meant it or not. "That means we should plan how to analyze the Van Allen radiations for a cure or anti-toxin agent against the Bug, and..."

"Wait," said Lloyd with a new note in his voice. "Come to my office. I want you to hear a tape we found in your spacecraft."

Mystified, Durk went up the elevators from his molelike headquarters underground, up to Lloyd's airy office in the BWB building. Lloyd turned on a tape recorder. Only a hiss sounded at first.

"This tape was connected to an electromagnetic sensor that probed space in the attempt to detect the Bug, or its spores, floating in space. It never did, but it picked up something else..."

The tape's hiss suddenly changed to a weird gabble.

Durk sat up, astounded. "It almost sounds like a voice."

"Doesn't it?" breathed Lloyd. "But a non-human voice. What do you make of it?"

Durk was silent. His whole perspective suddenly changed, in one great upheaval.

"Aliens!" he hissed. "What if the whole Brain Blight is a plot engineered by aliens from some other planet in outer space?"

Lloyd was staggered by the sudden, unexpected concept. "But how… why… where…" Confusion turmoiled in his mind.

Durk snapped his fingers in disgust. "It was in front of our nose all the time. What is the easiest way to conquer a planet if you don't want to or can't destroy all its inhabitants?"

Lloyd looked dumb and Durk answered himself. "By systematically wiping out its *leadership*. Once they are gone you have only a headless social organism to deal with, whom you can easily subdue and take over for its supply of workers or slaves. Don't you see the beauty of it, Lloyd?"

"Beauty?" echoed Lloyd, his thoughts unable to keep up with tills blinding revelation.

"In one stroke," continued Durk, his eyes blazing in newfound enlightenment, "that explains all the unorthodox mysteries of the Bug 'epidemic.' How it came out of nowhere… why it strikes high-IQ brains so selectively… why there are indications of intelligent planning behind it… and all the rest. Now it makes sense."

Lloyd was chewing his lip. "Whoa there. I'm not so sure. It doesn't explain at all how the disease is transmitted from brain to brain."

"Yes, it *does* explain that," rasped Durk. "Indirectly at least. By the very fact that this epidemic has *no* way of being transmitted again points to something unusual, something medically impossible. And that in turn points to some amazing way in which the aliens can 'inject'—how I don't know—the virus into human brains. We should have suspected it immediately," he said again in disgust. "It was so *obvious*."

He paused, then: "No, it wasn't, really. We can't blame ourselves for being stupid. The aliens cleverly modeled their campaign after an earthly epidemic. They could just as easily, I suppose, have attacked high-IQ people by shooting them down from space with a laser or something. By cleverly camouflaging their murderous campaign to simulate a contagious disease, they aroused no suspicions. A cunning red herring that fooled the whole world."

Very soberly he added, "We're obviously dealing with high-IQ aliens… very high-IQ."

"I don't know," Lloyd was saying doubtfully. "It's all a wild guess so far. It listens good but we're not sure at all that's the answer. Look, the garbled voice on the tape could be simply a distorted reflection of earthly radio voices…"

Durk snapped the recorder controls and ran the tape back for a replay of the portion with the enigmatic voice. "Listen, just listen," he demanded. "That's no human voice, no matter how distorted. It's weird… uncanny… *alien.*"

Lloyd nodded after a moment. "You're right, Durk. The question is, where did it come from? Where are the aliens located, in space?"

"Probably nearby," speculated Durk. "I doubt they could do a precision job of 'infecting' individual brains on earth from their home world which might be hundreds or thousands of light-years away. Logically, they're fairly close to earth, probably in some giant orbiting spaceship kept out of range of our tracking facilities."

"How can we ever locate it in that case?" said Lloyd, distressed. "Once we spotted it, we could shoot up nuclear missiles or armed satellites and blow them into the next dimension. But orbital space is big… big! How can we find them?"

Durk pointed at the recorder. "Maybe from that tape. Does it have more than one transmission of the alien voice?"

Lloyd nodded. "The space-program people who first ran it off said the voice periodically came in strong, then faded."

"Hmm. That means each time my spacecraft—while I was frozen— passed *under* the aliens much higher up but on the same side of earth, it caught their transmissions." His voice crackled. "Rush the tape back and have them put their top experts on analyzing the timing of the voice recordings. Maybe they can compute the exact point in space. It may be hard," he went on reflectively, "if they in turn are mobile. That is, if they move their craft about from orbit to orbit. In that case, it'll take some terrific calculations on relative and changing orbits to get a line on them. But it's worth a try."

Lloyd hesitated. "Shall we tell them what we're looking for? It'll be a shocker. And if we turn out wrong, we'll be utter fools."

"We have to take that chance," muttered Durk. "No help for it. But why stick our necks out? The space tracking outfit doesn't have to know what we're looking for, precisely. Tell them we just want to know the source of those peculiar transmissions. Don't even call it a voice. And slap a top security tag on it so they can't ask questions."

Lloyd stabbed at an intercom button that would summon a guard. After being given terse instructions, he walked out with the tape.

Then Lloyd and Durk looked at each other, still shocked themselves at this new and fantastic twist to the Brain Bug mystery. From a deadly but natural killer-disease, it had turned into another mind-staggering kind of deliberate killer.

Invasion from outer space, in a devilishly cunning way…

Durk broke the silence. "Regardless of how that turns out, we still have to carry out our original plan—for me to ride into space again and determine just how the Van Allen Belt radiations can bring immunity against the Brain Bug. If the aliens can't be directly defeated or destroyed, we'll still have that to fall back on."

"I'll make all the arrangements for the launch. But Durk, shouldn't you have help along? A team of scientists, experts in various phases of radiation physics and biology? I can order down one of our big space stations that holds six or more men."

"No," said Durk with a strange gleam in his eye. "There has to be a big laboratory aboard. And a two-man team will be enough—myself and Dr. Wayne Durk."

"Your recreate?" gasped Lloyd.

"Why not? With due modesty but going by the facts, we are the two men with the highest IQ left on earth. And we both happen to be bio-experts well versed in the use of radiations of all kinds in the study of germ or virus mutations. Yes, my double and I are the best bet to crack the immunity nut up there in space."

Irrelevantly, an old time song drifted into Durk's mind—*Me and My Shadow.* But it would be a very substantial "shadow" that would fly into space with him.

"Notify Dr. Durk at the Virology Lab," said Durk to Lloyd. "How soon can they set the launching?"

"On a top priority basis—which the Brain Bug project always gets—I would say in three days."

"Good enough." Durk had a sudden thought. "Have them equip our ship with the same sensor I had that picked up the unknown voice, plus any directional radar gadgetry they can think of. If analysis of my former tape fails to put the finger on the aliens, my twin and I can try."

CHAPTER 12

That night, Durk wandered in the cool of the evening, too charged up to sleep. The city's hum was slowly dying and its lights were flickering out. The dark skeletons of skyscrapers pierced into the star-flecked sky.

Events had taken a weird turn lately. Not only had he given "himself" a transfusion to save his double's life, but he and "himself" would soon embark on a space mission. His life seemed inextricably bound up with his recreate, so that they were thrown together more and more. Durk would have much preferred it the other way around. But circumstances were weaving a strange web involving the two men who were one man.

And now the most mind-numbing twist of all—that very likely aliens were behind the Brain Bug menace, seeking to demoralize a whole world to the point where taking over would be easy. A civilization deflowered of its genius and leadership would be ready prey for conquerors from space. The masses, with no one to turn to for intelligent guidance, would offer little organized opposition. Even to handle an army or a fleet of planes or a rocket missile system required key brains—which would be missing if the Brain Blight went full course.

Clever... cunning... fiendish.

Entirely the opposite of the usual concept of a vast armada of mighty space warships blasting down civilization in a crescendo of super-scientific warfare. This was a sneak attack, a subtle infiltration, an undermining campaign that would first weaken earthly resistance to the vanishing point.

In the final analysis, it was the power of the mind alone that made any civilization powerful and unconquerable. Subtract that top-grade mindpower and nothing was left that could face a determined enemy. If they ever succeeded in decimating earth's IQ-power, the remaining billions of leaderless and confused human beings would fall a prize to the aliens. And without a shot fired—or very few—the vast paraphernalia of civilization would be left intact, easily refitted and repaired into a smooth worldwide system by high-IQ overlords from another planet.

It was a cold merciless plan but a superb one, Durk had to admit. It was super-genius from the stars, relentlessly carrying out the downfall of an entire world after civilization had been made to fall apart like a rotten egg.

And could this mad-genius enemy be detected and defeated? There lay the great unknown. A huge shadow of uncertainty loomed over Durk, and he shivered from more than the night breeze.

Durk's preoccupation was shattered suddenly as he paused to light a cigar, then caught sight of movement behind him out of the corner of his eye. Sudden panic swept over him as he made out a dark form lurking in a shadowed doorway.

Durk moved on, glancing back as casually as he could. The dark form remained glued to his trail. Durk glanced wildly up and down the street. Like a fool he had wandered into a shoddier section of the city. Not another soul was in sight.

Abruptly, the dark form darted forward and closed the gap between them. Durk broke from a state of paralysis and started to run. But the pursuer sped up and a hand grabbed Durk's coat, holding firmly.

Durk remembered the time in the bar when tough men had looked him over and asked who he was. The Anti-Brain Movement… were they after him? Wildly, Durk tried to strike the man but met nothing. The man easily applied a Judo hold, bringing his face up close to Durk's.

"Easy, sir," he hissed. "I'm your bodyguard."

"Huh?"

"World Security Police, sir. You've been trailed by us ever since you contacted Finnegan Lloyd and took over a security post." He eased his hold on Durk's arm. "Sorry, sir."

Durk's relief left him limp, and his pulse stopped hammering. "Well," he said in a voice that shook a bit, "it's good to know I've got a nursemaid."

"Yes, but there's trouble brewing," muttered the operative, darting apprehensive glances around. "Our agents, infiltrating among the ABMen, got the tip that they are out to seize you, at the first opportunity. You've been under their surveillance too. We had better get out of this neighborhood immediately, sir…"

His voice ended in a gurgle as he arched his back with an agonized face. As he fell, Durk's horrified eyes saw the knife sticking in his back, obviously thrown from hiding.

Then Durk froze as dark menacing forms in rough clothing appeared out of shadowy places and slowly converged on him. He was boxed in.

"Don't move, mister," advised one of the men, holding a knife poised in his hand expertly. Durk did move. He bargained on one thing—they did not want to kill him but wanted to take him alive—for information about Recreate Labs. He remembered the elaborate security system Finnegan Lloyd had set up to keep the place a secret from all the world—and particularly from the ABMen.

Propelling his tall body powerfully, Durk took the nearest man by surprise and bowled him over with an elbow to the chin. Another man clutched for him. Durk planted a solid blow in his stomach and he doubled up in agony.

The way was clear now. Durk ran, fearing to look back. Would they hurl a knife after all, or shoot, rather than let him escape? He could almost feel the cold steel plunging into his spine from the rear…

But instead, a hidden man suddenly stepped out of the shadow, directly in front of him. A massive fist cracked into Durk's jaw. He went down for the count.

When Durk's senses swam back out of a black pit, bright lights hurt his eyes. A spotlight was trained on him and he was propped up in a hard chair. Dimly, he could make out men, many of them, behind the light's glare. They were in a huge old hall that had seen better days, the wall-paint peeling all over.

A hand slapped his face stingingly. "Snap out of it," said a gruff voice, issuing from a hard face overhung with unkempt hair, and breathing out the fumes of stale beer.

The tone changed to sarcastic politeness. "Welcome, Dr. Cecil Wright. Welcome to our headquarters."

"The Anti-Brain Movement?" murmured Durk. He had to know.

"Smart, aren't you? I'm Beevan, chief of the ABM section in this area, see? Now look, we want information—about a place called Recreate Labs. Yeah, we got agents all over and we finally got wind of that place. Question—is it true you somehow make duplicates of brainies?"

Dark said nothing.

A big hand swung and double-slapped him, viciously. Blood began to dribble from a cut lip.

"Answer, pig!" snarled Beevan. Hands held Durk's arms so that he could not move as the hand again slapped him brutally.

"Yes," mumbled Durk. It could not hurt to say it since they already knew the answer.

"Where is it?"

Durk hesitated. That was the key question. But before Beevan's punishing hand could swing again, Durk looked up and shot out a question of his own.

"Tell me. What have you got against 'Brainies' as you call us? I've heard a little of how you harass people of high intelligence. Why?"

"*Why?*" thundered back Beevan. He turned to survey his men, jerking a derisive thumb back at Durk. He whirled. "I'll tell you why, chum. Because all you big brains have made a mess of things. That's why. Shortages of food, clothes, vehicles… everything. All around the world."

"But we didn't *cause* the trouble," protested Durk, astonished. "It's the *lack* of trained minds, due to the Brain Bug epidemic, that is leading to civilization's slow collapse."

"Bah!" spat back Beevan. "It isn't that at all. We're glad the Brain Bug is doing our job. Or it was doing our job until this here recreate program started. Now we gotta stop that or the world will be full of Brainies again."

Durk's astonishment grew. He hardly knew what to say. Finally, "Suppose you succeeded in eliminating all high-IQ people. What would happen to the world then?"

"We'd get along fine, us regular people," said Beevan promptly and with incredible conviction. "All through history, it's the brainy people that caused trouble, not the common people. Without you big domes around, life will be much better and sweeter, believe you me."

Durk almost gagged, trying to find his tongue and carry on this unbelievable conversation. "But machines, inventions, the advances of science—they all come from human genius…"

"All geniuses are madmen," burst in Beevan intensely.

"Do you really believe that?" Durk gasped.

"Do we believe it, men?" roared Beevan, turning to his audience.

An answering affirmative bellowed from their massed throats. Durk had a glimmering of what this phenomenon was—an organized mob, one that did not break up after violent passions had burst forth. This was a *chronic* mob that had reached a mind-maddened pinnacle of hatred for superior minds and whose passions had never ebbed. The slow running down of civilization around them was only a sign to them that the 'Brainies' had built a false structure, doomed from the start.

"But think once," said Durk with patient persistence. "If the brainy engineers who run automation machinery die out, who will run the machines?"

"We will," said Beevan blandly.

"Do you know what an electronic circuit is?" countered Durk, almost angry at this incredibly ignorant statement.

"Never mind all that garbage," yelled Beevan, waving his arms wildly. "Your slick talk will get you nowhere. You Brainies look down on us regular people. You think we're dumb. Well, we're a whole lot smarter than you think, and we'll run the world just fine when you're all gone."

"But how… *how?*" groaned Durk. He tried to go on but knew it was impossible to convince them that it took brains and high-IQs to perform the intricate behind-the-scenes activities that made the wheels of civilization go around. These men, much as dumb apes who had captured a human village, really and hopelessly believed they could step into the shoes of their intellectual brothers and do as good a job.

It was comical, yet infinitely tragic. It was similar in a way to how barbarian hordes had crushed the Roman Empire, blind to the superior system of their victims, and totally convinced they could run things "better" than the Roman overlords. At other times in history, the common people—as distinguished from the intellectual elite—had run riot against authority and wrecked the structure built by finer minds. Without remorse and without understanding. And they had no inkling, no insight, into the disorganized hell they were creating for themselves.

Beevan punctuated Durk's thoughts in loud boasting tones. "Looky, egghead. In every factory or plant there's a hundred of us to one of you Brainies. So who *really* runs it?"

CHAPTER 13

Durk gave up. Argument was useless against this ghastly logic. He saw now that the rumors were not exaggerated. As if the ravages of the Brain Bug were not enough, the Anti-Brain Movement had spread like wildfire through the world, further assuring the eventual disintegration of society and its technological foundation. The final result could only be chaos, starvation, deprivation, and savagery as the vast machinery of the modern world ground to a halt, never to be started up again in a low IQ desert.

None of this was snobbery in Durk's attitude. It was not being patronizing or condescending. It was just plain realism in judging the relative values of low IQ and high IQ minds. Certainly many people under IQ-125—which was still comparatively high—could invent and do ingenious things. But for the big breakthroughs in science, key executive jobs of macro-magnitude, and the massive problems of governmental planning, macro-minds were an absolute necessity.

Durk knew from his intense study of brainpower statistics that there were some 400 million people on earth with an IQ from 115 to 125, or some 6.6% of the human race. They had never been attacked by the Brain Blight. They held important positions all through society as doers and go-betweens and programmers.

But they were still unable to replace or substitute for their superiors in mental attainments. Brilliance could be roughly defined as starting at IQ-125 and genius at 150, ascending upward to a peak of 200 and over in rare cases.

Minor genius rating from IQ-140 to 155 comprised a mere five million souls out of humanity's six billions. Scintillating genius from IQ-155 upward had mustered no more than one million all told, or one in 6000 people.

This Class-A genius class had all been wiped out by the Brain Bug, in the past eleven years. With the sole exception of Wayne Durk and his recreated double.

A bad blow. Almost a mortal blow. But not quite. The brain-power from IQ-125 to 155 could still hold the fort and keep civilization viable if not progressive. The alien enemy undoubtedly knew these cold, hard figures. Hence their ruthless and admittedly ingenious plot to decimate human brains down to the critical level of IQ-125. And it was only the recreate program that could stave off disaster—unless the unknown brain-killers stepped up the rate to wipe out the recreates faster than they could be produced.

It was a statistical conquest of earth, based solely on available brain-power. Their prefrontal lobotomy of mankind's most soaring mentalities would, in effect, leave the masses in a state of spiritless apathy, no longer sparked by the piercing brilliance so necessary to the march of science and the advance of human thought.

All this had whirled, in digest form, through Durk's mind as he confronted Beevan, the champion of the "common man." Durk was abysmally aware that he could never convince Beevan or his cohorts of those telling figures. They would never accept the sheer mathematics of the mental masterminds that alone had lifted the human race out of its primitive state and alone had forged the basics of civilization.

Beevan went by gross numbers. In his mind, the 98% of the human race under IQ-125, who performed practically all the work of the world, really held up civilization. The tiny 2% proportion who were "Brainies," by their very small numbers, could not have any real effect on society. It was as simple as that in his conception.

He could not understand that it was like a giant, automated sorter of peas run by a few photoelectric cells, and then taking those photoelectric cells out. Or like an atomic battery weighing 30 pounds activated by a speck of thallium-82. With the speck removed, the rest of the battery was dead or dying.

The whole body of human society, since ancient times, had comprised everything including that tiny "radioactive" speck of masterful minds. Remove that master "gland" of society and an incomplete organism was left that would in due time run down like any animal deprived of its vital pituitary.

"Yep, you Brainies only muddled up things," Beevan was saying, glowering at Durk as if he were some kind of witch. "You invented the atomic bomb and dam near blew the world to hell."

But what about atomic energy plants, Durk wanted to screech, which today in 1998 furnish 80% of the world's electrical power needs?

"You Brainies cooked up anti-biotic drugs and kept the weak sisters alive, which overcrowded the world, see?"

Durk groaned within. Beevan's insane logic had picked only a tidbit here and there, totally out of context with reality, to indict the genius class. It was mob psychology elevated to shining truth. A cult of paranoids who at last had found out who had always persecuted them. And in true paranoid style, they were also sure they could run the world better without the Brainies to "interfere." Delusions of grandeur...

Beevan began to act like a prosecutor at a trial, lifting up a finger each time. "You Brainies sent rockets to the moon and Mars and wasted Billions and billions of the taxpayers' money."

And nothing of benefit might come of this, such as new understanding of the solar system's formation or the giant moon telescope already probing the universe, or the eventual possibility of planet engineering to make Mars a colony world for the expansion of the human race.

Inexorably another finger went up. "You Brainies in your labs first discovered narcotics and pot and LSD and other bad drugs to poison our kids. And how about—" another finger—"DDT and other bug juice that disturbed the... uh... *ecology*. Eh, how about that?"

Durk rolled his eyes heavenward. Now Beevan was a scientific expert spouting esoteric terms which he assuredly didn't understand in the least.

"And how about pollution?" thundered Beevan, jabbing a finger up emphatically. "With all your chemical plants and stuff you poisoned the water and air."

Durk at times opened his mouth. But before three words were out, he realized the utter futility of trying to tell a man how a radio worked when he didn't even know what a kilocycle was.

Beevan was running out of fingers and he threw both hands wide. "All, there's a thousand other things you Brainies did to bollocks up life for good people. But the worst thing of all..."

He paused dramatically and this time pointed a finger at Durk accusingly. "The rottenest thing of all was to start up your recreate program. *Making* more Brainies, in your lab. First of all, it's *sinful*."

He took on a pious look and Durk realized that religious fanaticism held its part in the Anti-Brain Movement, as it often did in any reactionary group. But the next statement from their chief really was a bombshell to Durk.

"You see, *God* sent down the Brain Blight to wipe out you Brainies to cleanse the world. Now you're going against His will and creating ungodly imitations of the sacred human form."

Durk writhed. Oh, God. Now he was an evangelist preaching against the black voodoo of science. So it had been during the Black Plague in the Middle Ages, when pulpits proclaimed it was the hand of God scourging the wicked. How little human nature changed from its unenlightened inertia through the ages.

Durk began to realize it *was* a trial. A trial by mob. And now Beevan acted the part of a judge as he boomed: "We give you one more chance to tell us where your Recreate Labs are. Talk—or else!"

Durk shook his head almost violently. Sick inside, knowing he was in the collective hands of homicidal maniacs, he had already vowed to himself he would not reveal the place and thereby kill all chances for the human race to survive against the Bug. And to save humanity—Beevan's kind.

Beevan turned to a bunch of his men lolling in chairs, as if they were a jury. One of them made the thumb-down gesture, with a coarse leer. Beevan turned to glare malevolently at the prisoner.

"I pronounce you guilty of being the Brainie in charge of Recreate Labs, and of refusing to reveal the location. I therefore sentence you to death!"

His face turned utterly fiendish. "Death by having your skull split open and your crazy brains splattered all over."

It was all a dazed blur to Durk after that. He was seized and chained to a flat table, legs and arms spread-eagled. A brawny workman, wearing a black hood like an executioner, stepped forward with a pickaxe. He made a few practice swings in slow motion, with the point aimed at Durk's head.

Durk tried to be glad. Tried to remember how bitter he had felt at returning alive from space. How he had hated the thought of living in a crippled world that was sinking into a pit.

He tried also to remember how his life as Wayne Durk was over. His lab, his home, his wife and kids were lost to him forever. He was Cecil Wright, forging a new and lonely life without roots, without love, without incentive.

But he couldn't feel that way anymore. His mission of running Recreate Labs had given him a new and vital incentive to live. That desperate bid to challenge doom had lifted him above himself and above all other considerations.

And where a few months before he would have welcomed oblivion, now his soul protested agonizingly.

He saw the gleaming point of the pickaxe, poised for its brutal blow…

A noise interrupted, from the far end of the big hall. Shouts arose. The sounds of stun-guns and more lethal weapons. The hall quickly became a battleground. Vaguely, Durk realized that a fictional cliché had incredibly come true. A rescue force had arrived at the last moment.

In his chained position, Durk could see little except much scurrying among the ABMen as they retreated. The tumult died down. Then Durk was looking up—in shock—into his own face.

"Dr. Wright. Are you all right?" said his double anxiously.

Hysterical laughter bubbled up in Durk at the unconscious pun. And more laughter at the ludicrous twist of being rescued by "himself." It was all a fantastic farce, a hilarious comedy.

Durk was quickly unchained. He sat up to see a band of Security Police handcuffing captured members of the ABMen.

"But Beevan and his lieutenants managed to slip away," said Durk's double ruefully. He brightened. "But the main thing was to save you."

Durk was puzzled. It could not be because he was head of the recreate project. That was top secret, unknown to his double. Then why…

His unvoiced thought was answered by the double. "You saved my life with that transfusion. Turn about is fair play, eh?" He said it lightly but Durk saw his torn clothes, the bruise on his cheek, the gash in his arm. The battle had been short but deadly.

"How did you find me?" wondered Durk.

The double answered casually. "The Security operative who was knifed in the back did not die immediately. He managed to whisper a few words into his ring-radio, picked up at HQ, telling where he was and how Dr. Cecil Wright had been captured by the ABMen."

He smiled strangely. "Oddly enough, I had just been talking to Finnegan Lloyd over the optiphone when he got the news from a Security man who rushed in. So I heard it all. And I had a hunch somehow that I could help find where you had been taken. I insisted on joining the Security force and we found the now-dead body of the knifed operative. But we still didn't know just where the ABMen had taken you. Their secret hideout was unknown."

The look in his face became stranger. "I then had a queer hunch. A very strong *feeling* which way they had taken you. It was almost as if some sort of ESP signal were coming from you, that I picked up."

The Durk-double suddenly stared intently at Durk. "We seem to have some strong rapport between us. Some sort of psychic bond, or affinity. I've been wondering why that is. Another thing—we look quite a bit alike…"

Durk held his breath. Did his double suspect the truth? Had he somehow divined that he and Durk were more than just casual lookalikes? Durk winced, waiting for his double to pop the forbidden question and thereby open up a Pandora's Box of ills that would blight all their lives, including Ellen and the children…

"Ah, well," said the official Wayne Durk airily. "They say everyone on earth has a double. We're just two accidental doubles who happened to meet."

Durk breathed again. His double had evidently laughed himself out of any significant denouement to the resemblance between them.

"To continue the story," went on the double, "my sixth sense or what-ever it was, led me to this old hall. I *knew* you were in here and told the Security men. They were skeptical until they routed out a guard who tried to sneak away. Then they battered down the doors and invaded the place. And here we are."

On the ride back in a police aircar, Durk tried to fathom the miraculous "psychic sense" that had led his double unerringly to the den of evil. Para-normal science had advanced to the point in 1998 where certain psychic phenomena were recognized as established. One of them was "automatic ESP" between identical twins. In many experiments, the twins though far apart could exchange telepathic impressions, pictures, even messages at times. So why not the same bond between "twins" who were more identical than those born from the same womb? Durk and his double were the acme of identical twins. Hence it was hardly unusual that a psychic rapport should exist between them, perhaps even stronger than that between nature-born twins.

Durk shrugged it off as something to ponder more deeply in the future. Right now, he wanted to put the horrid memory of the mock "trial" and his near-execution back of him and look forward to his vital space mission.

"Do you know," he asked, curiously, "about the space mission planned for us?"

"Oh, yes," the double nodded. "That was what Finnegan Lloyd was telling me on the optiphone. I understand we are to go into orbit through the Van Allen Belt to find out how its radiations gave you immunity from the Brain Bug. I'm glad you asked for me to go along. Two heads are better than one."

He meant it whimsically, smiling. But again, within himself, Durk had to suppress a burst of hysterical laughter. The two heads were really one.

The police aircar left them off at Durk's hotel. He invited his double to come to his room for a moment, to discuss their coming space mission. It was still night, or the early hours before dawn, and both knew they wouldn't sleep anymore.

Durk the double—Durk now thought of his recreate as Durk and him-self as Wright—was puzzled. "I understand you went into space a year ago and thereby gained immunity from the Brain Bug. That was the space mis-sion I was supposed to have…"

"I was your follow-up," said Wright quickly. "As soon as your launch aborted, they sent me up on the same mission."

Durk's eyes were on him, still clouded. "You didn't tell me that when you came to my lab and introduced yourself. You said you came from the Anzac Province."

Uh-oh, thought Wright. Thin ice. Go carefully now or the cat will be out of the bag.

"That was for security reasons," Wright said, narrowly watching his double. "Just why they keep such things relating to the Brain Bug so secret I don't know. But they told me to tell no one of my space trip, just as you were told to tell no one when you thought you'd go up."

Durk grinned briefly, indicating he accepted that. Then another look of doubt came in his face. "That launch abort. They told me the launcher malfunctioned at the pad and was shut down before it could explode. But my escape tower system went off and yanked me miles away. They told me it landed with a severe bump that gave me amnesia. I didn't remember a thing until I awoke in the hospital."

And that moment of awakening had really been the double's "birth," Wright reflected. It had been a week after Durk-Wright's actual launch. After he had been lost in space, they had run off his life-tape—the first one ever made—and formed his recreate. Before revitalizing him and bringing him to sentient life, they had rushed him to a regular hospital. Finnegan Lloyd had met him there at his awakening, telling him the cover-up story. Lloyd, in a flash of brilliance, had seen how the double could replace Durk both at the lab and at home, saving heartache for Ellen and the children.

Wright-Durk was thankful for this, in a way. But he saw that Durk—just as he himself would have been—was not quite satisfied with the story.

"A week's amnesia," Durk was saying, as if it stuck in his craw. "But why did the amnesia blot out every bit of the launch event in my mind? And only that? I remembered everything clearly up until the last final physical I had."

At that final "physical" the life-tape had been secretly made, carrying with it all of Durk's memory up to that point—but *no further*. Hence, the "amnesia." It was a part of Durk's life he had never lived at all.

"If I were an expert doctor," shrugged Wright, "I'd try to explain that peculiarly 'selective' amnesia you had, Durk."

Durk seemed not to hear. "And I was in the hospital a week—a whole week—before I came to. If a man is in a coma that long how can he wake up so... so *healthy?*"

Yes, that had been the rub, Wright could see. Durk had not really been injured at all at the fictitious abort. When he had come to, he had felt like a well man without any injuries or feelings of illness at all. No wonder the matter preyed on his mind. It had been a makeshift cover-up at best, to keep him from knowing he was merely the recreated double of a presumed dead man.

"Why bother your head about it?" admonished Wright. Suddenly, he knew a way to clear those dangerous thoughts out of Durk's head.

"Finnegan Lloyd didn't tell you about our *other* mission?"

Durk looked surprised. "What other mission?"

"The second reason we're going into space," said Wright, slowly and deliberately, "is to detect the alien enemy who caused the Brain Rot epidemic on earth."

"Alien enemy…?" Durk looked thunderstruck.

There, thought Wright, that shocked the other topic out of his mind.

Wright then ran through the clue of the voice-tape and his two-plus-two deductions leading to an outside agency as the only acceptable explanation for the Brain Bug anomalies. Durk's face showed a wave of surprises that almost left him panting at the end.

"That changes the whole picture," Durk exclaimed, getting up and pacing the room. "It may be more important for us to locate the enemy's base, if we can, while in space. Then we can blast them out of existence."

"But suppose we can't blast them out of existence?" parried Wright, shaking his head. "Then our only chance is immunity to the Brain Bug. That's why our first job in space will be to hunt down that immunity factor."

"That makes sense," Durk conceded. But Wright could see that his brain was still afire with the amazing revelation of the aliens planning a diabolic sneak conquest of earth, using brain-bugs instead of bullets.

"Launch is scheduled in three days," said Wright, in a practical tone. "We'll start tomorrow ordering supplies and equipment to go up with us in a full-scale bio-lab. They're allocating us a six-man space vehicle with plenty of spare room."

CHAPTER 14

"Green and go," came the thin voice from earth-base to the two-man spacecraft. "You're in earth orbit. Perigee, 200 miles. Apogee, 10,500. Inclination to equator, 10 degrees."

"Roger," said Durk-Wright into his throat-mike, in the time-honored response of the first astronauts. "All conditions go aboard. Out."

He turned to Durk, his double. "We chose the equatorial orbit as that will swing us up directly into the Van Allen 'doughnut' that circles earth's equator. We'll have plenty of chance, in the next week, to test out which specific radiations are responsible for my immunity to the Brain Bug."

Wright was already opening the cases holding Brain Virus cultures. They had been rushed from dying scientists stricken by the blight. From previous studies, the BV-IQ survived as long as fresh brain-matter was supplied to them. Gruesome though it was, yet not shortening the lives of the doomed men at all, a large portion of undamaged brain tissue had been used to make up the virus cultures.

As their spacecraft began to slant up into the Van Allen zone, Durk adjusted their zeta-microscope and Wright fastened the first culture "slide" of living viruses under the lens.

"We don't quite know the mechanism of my immunity," said Wright. "Did Van Allen radiations somehow make my blood toxic to the brain virus? Did it create antibodies? Or did it become locked-up in white or red corpuscles, giving them the power to overcome the virus?"

"We'll have to test all possibilities," agreed Durk, peering into the microscope's eyepiece as they entered the lower portions of the Van Allen Belt, some 1200 miles above earth. "We'll use the sealed blood-samples— of other people than ourselves—to find out if anti-bodies are produced, or whatever, that will kill off the Brain Bug cultures."

"Meanwhile…" said Wright. He reached and snapped on the scanner of the EM-sensor that had detected the alien voice in his previous trip. "Meanwhile, we keep this on all the time until we pick up the alien voice again, in hopes of tracking it to its source."

Hours went by, then days.

They had to work in zero-g, of course. Wright was experienced in it from his previous orbital journey plus his pre-flight training. But he noticed with wonder how Durk also handled himself without difficulty, floating from instrument to instrument. Yet he himself had never had the least training for zero-g. He had been brought to life *after* Durk-Wright's training period a year ago.

But his duplicated mind also held the duplicated *memory* of that training period in zero-g simulators and diving jets. All the nerve responses to the lack of gravity were embedded firmly in his brain so that he handled himself just as surely as Wright himself, in freefall. It was another uncanny aspect of the whole recreate program.

"The 30th culture," muttered Wright. "Will it work?"

Durk was removing the blood sample from its receptacle outside the hull of the spacecraft, where it had been bathed in the Van Allen radiations. Drops were added to a Brain Virus culture and placed under the zeta-microscope.

Wright lifted his head wearily after ten minutes. "No go. The Brain Bug is feasting away on brain tissue, as chipper as a chipmunk."

Durk looked discouraged. "We've used filters to bathe each blood specimen in a different portion of the Van Allen radiation spectrum. We've subjected them to both the proton-type voltages and the electron-type."

"And we still," finished Wright, "don't get anything that even ruffles the hair of the Brain Bug. Damn blast!"

Durk's head jerked around. "What did you say at the last?"

Alarm bells rang in Wright's mind. He shouldn't have been so careless.

He didn't answer but Durk said, "*Damn blast*, you said. The very expression I use in extreme frustration. I've never heard anybody else ever use that term…" His burning eyes were on Wright, probing, questioning.

Wright laughed, easily. "I don't know why you're so concerned but before I visited you at the lab that time, Finnegan Lloyd briefed me on you. Said that if I heard a 'damn blast' from the lab before I walked in, I should quietly turn around and go. He said you would be in a terrible snarling state. The expression just happened to pop into my head just now, you see."

Maybe Durk saw, and maybe he didn't. Wright wasn't sure. Was fuel being added to his suspicions and was he gradually coming closer to the big secret of their dualship? Wright crossed his fingers.

Durk bent over the cultures. "Are you married, Wright?" he suddenly shot out.

Wright-Durk was completely taken aback. His mouth hung open but luckily Durk had not turned. He got hold of himself, mind whirling in a sea of emotions.

"No," he finally got out. "Never got around to it, somehow."

"Pity," returned Durk, still fussing with the cultures. "A man doesn't know what he's missing until he gets a wife, a good wife. Taken Ellen, now, my wife…"

Wright felt as if stabbed by a knife. Grimly, he clamped down on his quivering nerves, forcing himself to react neutrally.

"She's simply wonderful," said Durk, as if goaded by devils to torment Wright. "It's great to come home each night and find her waiting with her warm smile."

Wright refused to let the image come into his mind, clenching his jaw.

"Then the kids," went on Durk, as if conversationally. "Ah, children let a man relive life, seeing things all over again with their fresh young eyes. Wendy is five, a bundle of cuddly love personified. Randy likes me to pal with him at times, playing ball or going fishing. Great, man. It's as close to heaven as we mortals can ever get."

And it was close to hell to lose them, Wright groaned inwardly. No, it was hell itself. Was Durk just haphazardly talking about his—about *their*—family? Or was he deliberately needling Wright-Durk, trying to pierce his armor? Was he on the track of the recreate secret and determined to bring it out in the open?

But the Durk double must never know that he was not the real father of Randy and Wendy…

Wright began to wish he had never suggested his double as his space partner. Sure, it meant two ace brains working at the same problem, but he should have foreseen that thrown in close contact like this for days, significant things were bound to come up. Durk must have seen over and over how many gestures Wright made that were his own. Must have heard the familiar inflections in his voice that nobody could disguise. Could Wright still parry all suspicions and keep the bombshell from blasting his double wide open, if he ever knew the truth? At the very least, it would be a battle of wits to prevent the holocaust.

But Durk was not through.

"To change the subject," he said—but *was* he changing the subject? "I've heard strange rumors that certain men miraculously reappear again, after they die of Brain Rot. Do you suppose that could be true, Wright?"

Wright almost gagged. But he could see how it happened, those rumors. Even though the numbers of recreates were few so far, and well scattered around the world, here and there former acquaintances of the dead scientist would bump into his recreate—and wonder. The recreates, of course, had different names and were well schooled in covering up the connection, but people would still be puzzled and spread the story.

"Rumors are always what they were about anything—worthless," returned Wright as casually as he could, as if the matter were trivial.

"True, except for one thing," Durk went on while drawing a blood sample. "The other day I met a man who looked exactly like Pulsudski, the cytologist I lost last year to the Brain Bug. His exact double. I couldn't help stopping him and asking who he was. He gave some other name. When I mentioned who I was, he said he never heard of me or my lab. But still... his *living breathing double...*"

Wright cursed Finnegan Lloyd for not having transferred Pulsudski's recreate to another city or to the other side of the world, after he was brought to life. By blind chance, Durk had met him, further inflaming his suspicions about an unknown mystery that he was obviously trying to get to the bottom of.

Wright desperately tried to think of a response to what Durk had last said, something to pass it off effectively and put Durk off the track. He could think of nothing.

But he was saved the trouble. The EM-sensor suddenly began hissing as if something had been picked up. Then again, as on the voice-tape, Wright heard the sibilant gibberish of alien speech. And again, icy chills ran down his spine at the non-human tone, bringing instant revulsion to the human ear.

Durk also reacted, jerking around and stiffening with a look of loathing in his face. He waited until the short gabble faded out, then spoke in a nauseated whisper. "So that was the alien voice you first heard. I was wondering if it was your imagination that you immediately *knew* it was alien. Now I have no doubts."

Wright had been scribbling down coordinates from their orbital chart. "I've got the exact orbital position when the voice was at its loudest, which should be when their craft or space base is directly over us. This won't mean anything, however, as naturally they have a different orbit crossing ours only at two points. We'll have to get further readings before we can pinpoint their exact position and true orbital data."

"Keep the set open day and night," advised Durk grimly. "This may be more important in the long run than our immunity mission."

"I'll buy that," returned Wright, and a welcome idea worked its way into his mind. "And why don't we take turns sleeping so that one of us will always be awake when the next voice pickup comes. Each time, we'll have to work fast to get the exact space coordinates."

"Agreed," snapped Durk without hesitation.

Wright rubbed his hands mentally over his little trick. That way, one sleeping and one awake, they would have little chance to talk to each other—little chance for Durk to keep on prying into the nest of snakes about recreates.

Their work went on, under this split routine. Each was completely the equal of the other—and why wouldn't they be, Wright chuckled wryly to himself—in handling the blood-samples and tests by himself.

It was during Wright's vigil awake that the EM-sensor again reacted and picked up the weird syllables from nowhere. He recorded the coordinates and puzzled over them, but the data were still inadequate to pin down a point source in space. It was like tracking a new comet or asteroid. Astronomers required at least three good trajectory readings before they could roughly outline the full orbit and the object's position at any given time.

During Durk's next awake period, he too obtained a reading. He was too excited to let Wright sleep and shook him awake. "Look. The third coordinate readings. What do they match up with?"

Durk obviously had come to the answer already. Wright studied the figures. "Hmm. Signals came in only on one side of earth. Periods are a multiple of our own orbital period. Is the object standing still or—" he peered out the port window—"ah, the *moon!*"

Durk nodded. "Our three-hour orbit takes us under the moon eight times a day. But due to the different inclinations of our orbit and the moon's orbit to earth's equator, we only crossed line-of-sight paths once a day for three days."

Wright took a tremulous breath. "It means that the aliens have a base on the moon. We have bases there too, set up since the 1970's by both Americans and Russians, now under TWU jurisdiction. But they're tiny dots on the moon's surface, which is largely unexplored. The aliens could easily have a camp there, perhaps underground, that earth never detected or even suspected."

"And the voice transmissions," said Durk, adding his part to their rapid analysis of the find. "They might be a communications link between the moon and one or more spacecraft that reconnoiter earth, as part of their unknown method of implanting the Brain Bug in high-IQ minds."

"The theory," added Wright soberly, "is now 98 percent proven. An alien voice… and a source on the moon. Pretty good evidence that an enemy is at work against our planet."

Wright snapped on the earth-link radio. "Calling base. Brain Bug calling earth…" He kept it up for a while, with no answer. "Odd. Can't raise them. Is it space static or…"

Their eyes locked, widening.

Durk finished the thought that had sprung simultaneously into their minds, as thoughts inevitably must. "Or did the aliens *block* our message, not wanting that vital information relayed to earth, to start our military forces into planning an attack on their moon base?"

"That brings up an even graver thought," took up Wright. "That the aliens have somehow been *monitoring* us all along. They know we're in orbit…"

"And do they know what for? Finding the Anti-Brain Bug radiation?"

Wright stared solemnly at his double. "If they do, we may be in danger of attack by them. The question is, do we take no chances and deorbit immediately? Or…"

"The *'or'*," said Durk flatly, and it was an echo of the determination that already had filled Wright's mind. "We stick it out until we find what we want."

Wright-Durk found it uncanny. Their whole conversation had sounded exactly like carrying on a dialog with himself. Every reaction in his double, every leaping thought ahead, had been an echo of his own mind.

And at fleeting moments, Wright-Durk had become confused and asked himself—*Am I really the original? Maybe I'm the double and don't know it.* It scared him, until he took comfort in the fact that he alone had memory of the previous space trip a year ago. That was something his double could not have. Identity restored firmly, Wright-Durk felt better then.

CHAPTER 15

They had only two days left in their mission. As their craft grandly ascended in its eccentric orbit toward its peak each three hours, they passed through the Van Allen Belt and frantically tried every trick of viral pathology to find the golden cure for the Brain Blight. In what indefinable way had the radiations given Wright-Durk immunity, in his other trip?

They were still on a man-off man-on routine, each when awake apprehensively looking out into space for any alien vehicle approaching. When a rough hand shook Wright out of sleep the second day, he was sure the worst had happened.

But Durk's face was beaming. "We've got it," he sang triumphantly, holding up a culture tube. "The Brain Bugs all keeled over. Blood sample T-48 did it, irradiated by electron emission in the Belt at 66 BEV. All recorded by the bio-computer. Under the microscope I saw energized phagocytes attack and kill the virus."

"White blood corpuscles given a bio-electrostatic charge, eh?" gloated Wright. "The Brain Bugs simply get electrocuted. Now we've accomplished both parts of our mission. And the thing to do is…"

"Deorbit immediately," finished Durk, with another anxious glance out the ports. "There's one trouble. We haven't raised earth-base for two days. How will they know we're coming down, and where, for the pickup on earth?"

"No sweat," said Wright. "They've still got us tracked. The minute we retrothrust and start coming down, they'll know it and computerize our landing spot. And no matter where it is on earth, a pickup team will be there by plane, hovercraft, sub, rocket, or what have you. Whether on land or sea. A far cry from the early spaceflights when astronauts had to land at predetermined sites—or else never be found."

After the electronic check-out system pronounced all rockets and firing mechanisms go, Durk gave the countdown to retrothrust. "Three… two… one… fire."

Wright flipped the toggle. Nothing happened. He flipped it again and again, uselessly. Then he saw the red light blinking at the tab marked—FIRING MALFUNCTION.

"But why?" he hissed, "when a moment ago no malfunction was found by the check-out.?"

Durk turned a shocked face. "It can only be *interference*. From an outside source."

"From the aliens," whispered Wright.

Two ashen-faced men faced each other, in mutual dread.

And it hardly surprised them later to see a blip on their radar screen, of another object approaching. Wright turned swiftly to Durk. "This former six-man space station, as you know, is equipped with a life-rocket for one man to escape in, in case of danger. You're it. Hurry!" Wright was already shoving his double toward the small torpedo-shaped craft with a bubble-top nested in the rear of their lab space. "The life-rocket's hypergolic fuel needs no spark to set it off. It's unlikely that the aliens can interfere with its retrorockets. You can deorbit and land on earth." He dumped in their notes on the anti-blight radiations. "Deliver these to earth. The radiations can be duplicated in labs to give immunity to all the high-IQ people on earth. Get going."

"Why me?" protested Durk.

"Because I say so," commanded Wright tersely. "I'm the flight commander." He shoved his double into the open hatchway and slammed it shut. He snapped on a radio intercom. "I'll put on my spacesuit. Then you go."

Glancing anxiously at the rapidly approaching radar blip, Wright struggled into his spacesuit and clamped the helmet on, valving in oxygen. Then he nodded to Durk in the bubbletop and pulled a lever that opened a large door in the spacecraft.

With a roaring whoosh, the air rushed out of the larger craft, pulling the small life-rocket with it. With a last wave and forlorn look, the double turned on his retrorockets and the tiny ship fell behind and dwindled to a speck.

Durk—the original Durk—watched anxiously. Had the aliens detected the departure of the emergency craft? If so, could they do anything about it? Durk waited tensely, half expecting some ray or other weapon to span space and seek out the escaping life-rocket. But nothing happened and Durk grinned. By now, the rocket was arching grandly into its descent pattern, ready to plunge into earth's atmosphere. Maybe the aliens had frantically tried using their interference-beam to prevent the retro-fire and had been dismayed to find it didn't work, thus letting their quarry escape. Still, it didn't fit. With their fantastic speed—assuming the aliens had advanced flying ships—they could easily over-take the life-rocket. Well, they hadn't so they hadn't.

Durk felt a quiet satisfaction, no matter what he himself now faced. He had forced his double into the life-rocket not only to deliver their vital anti-blight data to earth, but to return to the arms of Ellen. If only one of them could return, it had to be his recreate. Durk himself, with his lack of a year's memory while lost in space, would have soon exposed the bombshell truth of the two men in Ellen's life, to her undying shock. This way, there had been only one man in her life as far as she knew, with the return of Durk's double from space. Far better that way.

Durk's spacecraft had no armament on board of any sort. It was strictly a scientific vehicle. He could only watch helplessly as the blip enlarged on the radarscope. Peering out, he soon saw it visually. A surprised grunt escaped his lips.

It was a flying saucer.

A disk-shaped craft quite similar to those that had mysteriously been reported on earth since 1947. The riddle of the UFO's, thought Durk wryly, had existed for some 50 years. It was now about to be solved.

The huge saucercraft angled in expertly. Durk flipped on his radio. "Calling craft X. Identify... identify." The answer that came back was the same weird gabble he had picked up before. That confirmed it in Durk's mind. It was the alien enemy.

Silently, the saucer wheeled and aligned itself flatwise with Durk's craft. Then some sort of pulsating beam of violet leaped from the saucer and seemed to grip Durk's craft like an intangible anchor. He felt his ship being yanked away, following behind the saucer. Durk could tell by the trajectory that their curving space path would take them to the moon. The puzzle was all falling into place, piece by piece. But many pieces remained to be filled in...

Durk removed his confining spacesuit after once more sealing the cabin and valving in oxygen. Might as well be comfortable on the ride to the moon as a prisoner. Down on earth soon, his double would be gasping out the story of the space ambush and how Wayne Durk had been captured by the unknown space enemy.

What would they do then? What *could* they do? Without knowing the exact spot on the moon where the alien camp existed, it would be a hopeless search. And earth in 1998 did not have spacecraft of war or any great numbers of search craft. Space travel was still too new. The chance of rescue,

Durk knew, was very nearly zero. He would be swallowed up in a big dark question-mark as far as earth was concerned.

What did the aliens want with him? If they had monitored his scientific activities and discovery of the anti-blight radiation, why not simply destroy their ship and its two occupants before? Why bring him in for interrogation? *If* that was their reason…

Durk's pulse was hammering as the saucercraft continued towing him at terrific speed and the moon loomed hugely before them within an hour. He was about to meet outer-space aliens for the first time in human history. People from some other remote planet in the vast depths of galactic space. People who had ruthlessly launched a disguised conquest of earth.

What would they be like? Human or otherwise?

The saucercraft swung into a new trajectory over the moon, with Durk's craft locked to it and following the same path. No visible rocket-blasts or any other sign of propulsion came from the saucer, but it suddenly decelerated with about 10-g's force, flattening Durk against his forward wall gaspingly.

Then the strain eased and Durk looked down at the lunar surface only a mile below. Their two locked craft now drifted gently down toward a broad crater. Amazingly, Durk saw the entire bottom of the crater suddenly lift up, like a lid. The saucercraft and its towed companion plunged down into the dark maw revealed.

Durk sensed the artificial crater-floor lid clamping down again, then another huge partition opening and closing, in airlock fashion. Now a blaze of light surrounded them and Durk had the impression of a vast underground cavern filled with flying craft of all kinds of different shapes. And all the walls of the cavern held hexagonal dwellings packed neatly together. There was an air of great bustle and activity.

Something flashed into Durk's mind, intuitively. It was like a beehive.

Durk felt a soft bump as his craft landed on something solid. Once more donning his spacesuit, Durk stepped out. There was no sense trying to hide inside his craft with the door locked. Now that he was in the enemy camp, he had an overwhelming desire to find out what it was all about.

The other saucercraft had also landed. Durk saw its hatchway swing open and waited for the beings to emerge, holding his breath. He gaped as he saw a group of short creatures file out, no more than 3½ feet tall. They had arms and legs and faces and were thus roughly humanoid.

But there the resemblance ended. They had three-fingered hands, and legs that seemed to have no knee-joint so that they waddled stiffly as they walked. They wore one-piece "diving suits." Their faces were the most peculiar, featuring a slit-mouth, a brief nose and two nostril-slits, and wrap-around eyes that extended from the front part-way to the side of the face.

Suddenly it leaped into Durk's mind. The classical description of the "little men" who had been reported to land on earth and step out of saucers, for the past 50 years. Obviously, then, they had been reconnoitering earth for that length of time, preparing no doubt for their Brain Rot coup that started eleven years ago. A long-range invasion carefully planned in advance.

One of the dwarfed aliens came up to Durk and opened his helmet, exaggeratedly drawing in a lungful of air, obviously to indicate it was breathable. Breathable for him but how about humans? Still, as the little man gestured for Durk to open his helmet, he decided to give it a brief try. As soon as the visor was open, he felt the wash of good air, perfectly suitable for human lungs. Thankfully, he took off his helmet and also unzipped his spacesuit. As with all spacesuits since those of the first astronauts, they were too confining and clumsy to keep on if not necessary.

Durk now looked around and his first fleeting impression of a giant beehive was confirmed. The entire wall space and sloping ceiling were occupied with the queer six-sided enclosures, in which Durk could see more little men behind small windows. All were the same, like the cells of a monastery... a million of them at least.

Durk heard footsteps and turned, startled. Approaching were entirely different creatures, eight feet tall, built powerfully, and having one single huge eye in the center of their foreheads.

Another kind of visitant from flying saucers, according to piled up UFO reports on earth.

Durk noted immediately that these giant creatures, with massive limbs and bulging muscles, were dressed in thin armor, plus various weapons slung in a belt, from a club-like affair to small metallic guns.

Something else sprang into Durk's mind—warrior "ants." Was this civilization a curious mixture of the bee and ant societies of earth?

The "warriors" had preceded another party and now formed two ranks. Durk really got a shock this time at the creature approaching. It was a human being, a normalized man with a handsome face and long golden hair. His movements were graceful and his clothing was elegant, including a scarlet tunic, royal blue skin-tight trousers, and a sash of gaudy colors. He also wore rings with flashing stones.

And again, Durk was reminded of the tales, seemingly fanciful, of people on earth meeting such "Greek gods." All UFO "legend" was coming true, here on the moon.

CHAPTER 16

The newcomer smiled and bowed with a flourish, "Her Majesty the Queen bids you welcome," he said and Durk started. It was perfect English. "I am Prince Ellgu. You will come with me, please."

The two ranks of warriors closed in beside Durk, giving him no choice but to follow the dapper prince. He led the way through an arched doorway into a sumptuous chamber. Sumptuous was the only word. Richly colored drapes hung on the walls. Furniture of some glowing plastic adorned the room and a sort of humming music that was strange but not unpleasant filled the air.

The prince threw himself on a lounge indolently and began popping what looked like small red berries in his mouth, from a bowl of crystal cut in intricate designs. It might be the luxurious chamber of an old-time king on earth.

"We live in luxury, we drones," said Prince Ellgu languidly.

"Drone?" echoed Durk, startled.

"Ah, yes. We have studied enough of earthly things to know that your ant and bee societies have a drone class. Also workers—the little men. And warriors, the big ones."

Durk's intuitive guesses had all been right. His mind made a leap ahead and he recoiled. "Your queen—?" he said hesitantly.

"You will see her later," said Ellgu, waving a hand. "Right now, one of my other duties is as Chief of Earth Watchers. A sort of espionage service, you might say. Our ESP-monitor, of course, followed your craft into space. When we read your thoughts and found out you suspected our existence on the moon, and also worked out the radiation-immunity… why, we then had no choice but to capture you."

"Then you are," burst out Durk, in sudden rage, "responsible for the Brain Blight among my people."

"Naturally," smiled Ellgu, rather smugly. "Clever, don't you agree? Our plan was simply…"

"I know your rotten plot," said Durk savagely. "To kill off all the high-IQ people on earth, leaving the masses, virtually leaderless and without science talent or the other qualities that gifted humans have. A cold-blooded scheme to murder brainpower on earth, leaving a headless civilization that is impotent."

"Correct," nodded the prince, unabashed.

"Then, when all the sparkplug brains of earth are gone, you would step in and take over the world, too disorganized to put up any effective resistance."

"What else could we do since we did not have the means to defeat you in warfare?" The prince grinned as if sharing a confidence. "Oh, we have an advanced technology. You know that from the fleet of scout craft—flying saucers and UFO's to you—that have spied on earth for 50 of your years. But we simply do not have the industrial facilities on our home planet, or here, to produce a mighty war fleet of conquest. Thus we had to use our wits and devise the subtle method of truncating human society's master brains to render your people helpless."

Durk wanted to rush to the sneering prince and choke him. With an effort, he controlled himself. His scientific curiosity now egged him to ask, "Just how did you create the Brain Blight? How could you make it work like a viral epidemic yet without any means for transmitting the contagion from victim to victim?"

The prince took on a look of boastful pride.

"One of our most ingenious tricks. During a stretch of 40 years—prior to the loosing of the epidemic—our 'little men' workers on earth landed in remote spots and set up certain devices in hidden places. They consist of a small tower with a mind-sensor. These mind-sensors, scattered over earth, could 'tune in' on individual minds and determine their mental rating. Their IQ, as you call it. In that way, we catalogued all the brilliant minds on earth through the years."

Durk saw now why they had been around for 40 long years before striking. It must have been a monumental task to examine and pinpoint over 100 million high-powered human minds, separating them from the billions of lesser mentalities.

"Once we had the IQ list completed, we used another advanced device whose workings I'm afraid you can never understand. To us, you know, even a brilliant scientist like you has a low IQ. I can only describe it to you in oversimplified terms."

"Get on with it," snarled Durk, smarting at the insult and yet miserably aware that the comparison of intellects might be true.

"First of all, our medical experts created the Brain Rot virus out of many mutations of a common virus know on earth, until it was deadly to any human brain."

"*Any* human brain, regardless of IQ?"

Ellgu nodded. "The secret is that we used our mind-probe, which could single out any individual brain on earth we wanted. It is too intricate to go into the 'tuning' methods which could focus on that brain, a quarter million miles away from us on the moon, even if that brain and person were moving about. But once attuned, we then *teleported* the virus directly into his brain." Durk gasped, speechless at the incredible feat.

"Yes, teleported," repeated the prince, proudly. "One moment it was here under the focus of the mind-probe. The next moment—whisk!—it materialized in the target brain."

Durk jerked to his feet and paced up and down, face working.

"That explains the fantastic spread of the epidemic—in a still more fantastic way. But I have to believe you. It's the only logical answer. So in that way, you were able, in the past eleven years, to start at the top of the IQ list and wipe out millions of major and minor geniuses on earth. Diabolical… heartless… fiendish…"

"Human words that have no meaning for us," shrugged Ellgu callously. "What else is one of our swarms to do when we must seek a new world?"

"Swarms?" Durk's mouth hung open. "You don't mean…"

"Quite like your bees and ants," nodded the prince matter-of-factly. "Evolution on our world worked differently than on earth. On our planet, the primitive species which was our 'missing link' was a bee-ant creature that evolved to intelligence, instead of a human species. Through the ages, swarming took place periodically, in the central home. That is, a new queen would be born who would fly away with her drones, workers, and warriors to seek another home-site."

"Literally fly?"

"Yes. During the swarming stage, due to special foods, we gain temporary wings that fall off after we have reached our new home. But then a problem came up…" Ellgu waved as though ages went by.

"There came the time, after many swarmings, when there was no place to swarm to. Our planet was filled, crammed, overcrowded. Wars rose, very bloody wars comparable to those in your history, some of which I've studied. So then…"

He paused dramatically. "So then we took the only alternative—*swarming into space.*"

"You've taken over other worlds before?" Durk could hardly hide his repulsion at the thought of ant or beelike creatures descending smotheringly on other civilizations, like horrid locusts.

"Many," agreed Ellgu blandly. "However, we could no longer fly with wings into airless space. But science and technology had arisen and the answer was simple—spaceships."

Durk marveled at the strangeness of it. A race of intelligent beings but with all the traditions and instincts of their bee-ant ancestors. A totally different sexual and reproductive system resulted in the overcrowding of each "nest" and led to the same kind of swarming that earthly bees, ants, and termites followed, age after age. The unique thing about Elgin's people was that by means of science technology, they had burst their natural bounds and could soar to other worlds. They had the universe as their swarming grounds...

Durk cut off his nauseated thoughts. "But why the brain-killing method of conquest? Why couldn't your science technology produce space war craft and super-weapons for conquering other planets?"

"There are several reasons," said the prince, ticking them off on his fingers. "First of all, the swarm that splits off is not numerous, no more than a million or so individuals. We are all crammed, incidentally, in this one lunar cavern, in our compact 'beehive' manner."

He grinned and went on. "Second, most of our citizens are born either dumb workers or equally brainless warriors. The elite thinking class, we drones, is limited. Hence, we never had the *spread* of science-technology that alone can come forth with powerful weapons and fleets. We could only concentrate on such esoteric science systems as the brain-virus teleported to aid us in conquest."

Durk could see how a rigidly regimented bee-society such as theirs allowed for little expansion of brainpower. On earth, all human parents contributed each generation to the genius pool. In Elgin's society, only a limited number of the humanlike drones with high intellect were born under their restrictive genetic pattern. And they apparently could not alter that anymore than medical science on earth had yet stirred the age-old genetic pot to increase IQ. Well-worn biological paths, perfected meticulously by nature through long eons, could not be easily changed whether on earth or any other world.

"Third," continued the prince, "the immensity and logistics of space swarming means a limited number of passengers. We had to leave the greater bulk of our workers behind, to be mercifully gassed. By our brain-virus system, we will find new workers on earth—your conquered people."

Durk felt like being sick and barely controlled himself. He wondered why the stark picture wasn't driving him mad. A depleted swarm of intelligent bee-people, needing billions of "workers" to carry on their menial tasks, enslaving a whole race of humans... horrible. And for this basic need of theirs, they were callously destroying all the finer minds on earth, those that had sent civilization and art and culture to sublime heights.

It was the most unfair and undeserving kind of conquest imaginable. Even a warlike race attacking earth with spitting ray-guns would shine as respected figures in comparison. This wanton destruction of great minds by the utterly egocentric bee-men cried out as a revolting crime against the universe.

Savagely, Durk wished he had some sort of bellows to pump smoke into this beehive of iniquity and exterminate them—like insects. They were, in a sense, parasites preying on nobler civilizations of free minds and substituting their gross antpile existence without human feelings or esthetics, like maggots wallowing in the carrion of a dead civilization.

Durk shuddered at the thought of other worlds of thinkers, seeking beauty and truth, already smothered by these crawling beehive beasts whose sole goal was perpetuation of their mind-crippled race.

It was cruel. It wasn't fair. It was ungodly. Durk was crying inside, crying in frustration and disgust and agony for all good minds in the universe, with this horrendous Armageddon facing them as more and more bee-people swarms went forth...

"What is wrong, earthman?" said Ellgu, genuinely puzzled. "After all, we are a superior form of life, since we are able to win out and dominate other races. Isn't that obvious?"

Yes, if might makes right, thought Durk. Or more to the point—if evil sabotage makes superiority.

The prince arose. "I just received an ESP call. Come. You are to have the privilege of meeting our queen."

Durk followed with trepidation, almost sensing the ominous revelation to come. Ellgu led him through a door flanked by monster-men warriors as guards, into a still more resplendent chamber hung with crystalline adornments and woven tapestries. Their society was a curious mixture of the beehive and the factory.

Then Durk's eyes sprang open and a silent cry of horror twisted his lips. Dominating the other end of the huge chamber was a gigantic figure. The upper end of it was tiny and vaguely human down to the waist. The rest was horror—a great swelling body with wormlike folds, as big as a house.

"Queen Torza," said the prince half-reverently, kneeling abjectly. "The mother of our swarm."

CHAPTER 17

He turned to Durk with shining eyes. "She has been fertilized and will be ready to produce millions of eggs—at the time earth falls into our hands."

"Eggs," said Durk, idiotically.

"They produce the normal quotas of workers, warriors, and drones."

"You," gulped Durk, "you came from an egg?"

"Didn't you?" retaliated the prince, maliciously. "Of course your egg was nurtured within your mother's body before you were born. In our case, the egg comes out and the person then hatches."

His stomach turning over, Durk had to run behind a curtain. He came away paler but feeling better. The hideous creature on her throne—no doubt beautiful in Elgin's eyes—spoke in a piping screech.

"I, too, know your language, earthling." Her humanlike face was cold, hard. "Prince Ellgu, shouldn't this creature be executed? Isn't he the one who caught onto our secret?"

"Yes, Majesty," said Ellgu. "But don't bother your regal mind with such base matters. We drones will handle it. We have another reason for capturing him alive. We want to know about the *recreates*."

Durk froze inside. He had wondered how much they knew.

"We have become aware through our saucer scouts that certain scientists who died with our Brain Rot suddenly appeared alive again. We can of course also teleport the virus into their brains as we've begun to do."

Which neatly explained, to Durk, the mystery of the seeming "immunity" of the recreates, at first.

The prince looked stern. "But we cannot have this recreate program— we picked up the name from your mind with our ESP-sensor—going on. Therefore, we must use direct intervention and destroy that place. Where are your Recreate Labs located?"

"Why don't you read my mind and find out?" sneered Durk.

"We will have to… ah, it is done." Ellgu pointed at a glinting lens shining some sort of ray from a wall recess. "The mind-probe extracted the information we want."

"Just like that?" gasped Durk.

"Just like that," said Ellgu flatly. "We are experts, you see, in telepathic science. Now that we know where the Recreate Labs are, a small force aboard a flying saucer-craft, armed suitably, will be all we need to make a sudden night raid. Your recreation program will come to an abrupt halt."

Ellgu smiled saturninely. "And since you will never return to earth, the data on anti-Brain Blight radiation giving immunity will never be delivered."

"But what about—" began Durk, then stopped. He had been about to ask about his double in the life-rocket. But it suddenly occurred to him that not once had Ellgu referred to the other Durk or his rocket.

Did that mean his double's escape had gone unnoticed?

Wild hope flooded Durk. But then he glanced in dismay at the lens pointing at him. Would the mind-probe extract and expose his secret?

But Ellgu noticed his glance at the mind-probe. "I have turned it off. We have the key information we want, about your Recreate Labs. Later, perhaps, our doctors will probe your mind more fully, to find out all about human thinking processes." He stared sadistically at Durk. "Yes, instead of exterminating you as the Queen suggested, we will keep you alive as a human specimen to be mentally dissected."

Durk shuddered in advance at horrors he could not even imagine. But his own fate aside, the important thing was if his double had reached earth safely. And if so—Durk was grinning within himself—the beemen were playing a losing game. Let them destroy Recreate Labs. What would be the need of recreates when the radiation immunity was known? The originals would never die. The aliens, even if not wiped out, had already been defeated—if his double had reached earth safely.

"By the way," said Ellgu conversationally as they left the queen's chamber, "the anti-Brain Bug immunity would have done you no good, even if you had delivered it to earth."

Durk's whole nervous system came to a screeching halt. "What do you mean?" he said hoarsely.

"We have other virulent strains of the Brain Rot ready. The moment we found the present strain ineffective, we would switch to another type, one that would be immune itself to your immunity remedy. And the decimation of your brainpower would go on."

At that moment, Durk very nearly went mad. All his hopes were smashed at one blow. His double's immunity data delivered on earth, even if he had escaped, would mean nothing. And if Recreate Labs were destroyed, earth's last hope went with it.

Earth was playing the losing game, after all.

Durk went into a state of dazed numbness in which he had no more feelings. All the universe seemed a grey fog in which he was lost, stumbling blindly. He was hardly aware that he was being led into a big white room, in which beemen drones like Ellgu were waiting with ghoulish smiles, surrounded by gleaming instruments.

Instruments of mental torture? Durk did not know and did not care. All he could think of was his double eagerly delivering his radiation immunity data—uselessly. A false hope that could never save the human race.

And what good would it be for his double to return home safely, to Ellen's arms? The recreate secret would still be unknown to them both, promising a happy life ahead. Happy? *When the world turned into a vast beehive…?*

* * * *

The double of Durk stood beside his landed life-rocket, somewhere in the Amazon jungle. For the first time since leaving the big spacelab, he breathed easier. All the way down during his flaming reentry, he had died a thousand deaths—from flying saucer attackers. But they never materialized. Like Durk on the moon, he was puzzled. Had his escape by rocket from their mother ship gone entirely unnoticed? It seemed incongruous somehow. If they knew two men were aboard, how could they let one of them slip away without challenge? Somehow, the pseudo-Durk sensed there was some inexplicable mystery here.

He swept those thoughts aside, expanding his lungs and drinking in fresh air gratefully after the canned air of the space mission. The life-rocket's automatic signal radio was beep-beeping merrily. Pickup should come soon.

Almost immediately, a tiny dot appeared in the air and slanted down toward him. It resolved into an X-77 rocket-plane that roared to a halt 500 feet high, then lowered smoothly on underjets, landing fifty feet away with scarcely a bump.

Three smartly clad members of the Space Rescue Service stepped out and saluted. "Tracking had you all the way, sir. Hop in. Finnegan Lloyd is anxious to see you in Earthia City."

It was night when they arrived but the fat chief of the Bureau of World Brainpower was waiting. "Only one of you," he greeted Durk, sorrowfully. "But of course only one man can squeeze into a life-rocket."

Finnegan Lloyd was playing for time, keenly looking over the other. Which one was it? Both had worn the same onboard fatigues of astronauts, as alike as peas in a pod. Remembering Durk's fierce and oft-repeated warnings, Lloyd did not want to greet him the wrong way. Durk or Wright? Which one was it?

To his relief, the returned man solved the dilemma. "Yes, Wright was left behind—at his own choice. He insisted I go."

"But what happened, Durk?" demanded Lloyd. "We're all in the dark down here. Two days ago all radio transmission between us blacked out. Then suddenly, our tracking people see the life-rocket leaving. They also caught another object approaching the spacecraft." Lloyd's voice went down to a low hiss. "Was it an enemy ship? Was Wright's theory right?"

Durk nodded and told the whole story. Then he dumped the briefcase he had brought along from the life-rocket onto Lloyd's desk. "Full data on Brain Blight immunity."

"Hurray," said Lloyd in a faint voice but fervently. He raised his eyes upward as an amen.

"Scratch one sneak invasion of earth." He started. "What's that noise?"

It came from the hall. Lloyd dashed to the door and swung it open. A horde of rough-clad men swirled by. "To the special elevators," yelled one man. "Then down to smash Recreate Labs!" The man was Beevan.

"It's the Anti-Brain Movement crowd," gasped Durk. Lloyd shut the door with a peculiar grin. At his desk, he snapped on the intercom connecting to the labyrinths below. "Guards," he commanded. "The ABMen are coming to wreck the place. Don't try to stop them. Let them have fun."

A surprised grunt came back and incredulous words. "Yes, I mean it," snapped Lloyd, still grinning. He clicked it off and turned to Durk. "Let them destroy Recreate Labs. We don't need it anymore." He held up the briefcase. "Not when we have this to save all other high-IQ people on earth."

Durk was standing transfixed. *"Recreate Labs?"* he whispered hoarsely. "Labs where dead men are recreated?"

But Lloyd wasn't listening. He was listening instead to the sound of muffled explosions from deep underground, that vibrated through the building squatting over the site. "Seems they came well prepared to do a thorough job. All the life-tape machines, the recreate cabinets, the computers—being blown to bits." He laughed uproariously. "And it doesn't matter a damn. The ABMen think they're winning their battle against the 'Brainies.' Think they'll take control of the world. But they don't know that no more brainpower will be lost and the world will be safely in our grip—for their own good. Stupid... stupid."

He was still shaking his head when the room shook violently and plaster came off the walls. "What are the fools using—nuclear charges?"

"No—look," yelled Durk, pointing out of a window. "A flying saucer is also attacking here."

CHAPTER 18

They stared open-mouthed as a huge silvery disk spun around the BWB building and unleashed some vibratory force that was shaking the structure to pieces.

"Out to my aircar on the balcony," shouted Lloyd and Durk followed him. They jetted away just as the building crumbled and sagged, collapsing into a broken heap that spread over nearby city blocks. The few night pedestrians and groundcar drivers around were crushed instantly.

Lloyd kept the aircar buzzing on high as they stared down in horrified fascination. Now the saucer lowered and aimed some kind of red beam which ate its way through the rubble.

"Looks like they're trying to get down to Recreate Labs," muttered Lloyd in a dazed voice, "as if they want to destroy it too."

Durk looked up, at the moon, in sudden intuition. "The aliens must have gotten the information out of Wright, as to the location of Recreate Labs. Naturally, the aliens would want to wipe it out."

Lloyd's eyes were stunned. "Of all the crazy coincidences. What a trick for fate to play. The ABMen and aliens, both wanting Recreate Labs destroyed—and both striking at the same time."

"That brings up a strange thing," mused Durk. "I just wonder what the ABMen will think when they see the aliens…"

And the moment would come soon. Peering down, they saw the saucer land and little men pouring out, clad in one-piece suits and carrying odd weapons. They clambered down into the holes their red beams had dug through the rubble, down into the maze of Recreate Labs.

The answer to Durk's question came an hour later. A dusty human figure followed by his men struggled up out of the rubble. It was Beevan. Lloyd lowered his aircar and landed nearby, running forward.

Beevan recognized him. "Finnegan Lloyd, chief of BWB." But oddly, there was no rancor in his voice. He jerked his thumb back and down, his eyes infinitely baffled. "Who were those little rummies that came below? We killed some and got out but *who were they?*"

Durk moved forward. "You're in for a big shock, Beevan. They're aliens, men from some other planet of some other star. They have a camp on the moon. It was they who sent down the Brain Blight, by scientific means. They wanted to wipe out human brainpower so they could come and take over the rest of humanity as slaves. Including you."

Beevan looked like he had received both barrels of a shotgun, not once but a hundred times. He swayed on his feet for a moment. The men behind him whispered back and forth in feverish excitement.

"This the straight goods?" said Beevan feebly, as if still suspicious.

"You *saw* the aliens yourself," returned Durk bitingly. "What more do you want?"

Below them came a crashing sound. Beevan pulled himself to his full height, a ferocious rage reflected on his face. "Those little crumb bums can't come to earth and wreck what belongs to us—to us humans." His voice rose to an almost insane screech. "Come on, men. We'll wipe 'em all out."

To a man, clutching clubs, guns, and grenades, they scrambled down the hole. There were over a hundred of them. There had been no more than twenty-five aliens.

"I don't think any of the little men are going to come out alive," murmured Lloyd. "Durk—"

He turned but Durk wasn't there. He was sprinting toward the landed saucer, and darted in its open hatchway. When Lloyd caught up and peered in, he saw Durk sitting in a curved chair before a bank of instruments and controls.

"Hmm, not too much different from the control panel of one of our spacecraft," he was mumbling aloud.

"Are you thinking of flying it?" gasped Lloyd. "Where?"

"To the moon." Durk turned a grim face. "Wright is a captive up there. I've got to get him free if I can."

"But you don't know *where* he is on the moon," protested Lloyd, as if to someone who had lost his reason. "If we did know, don't you think I'd have notified the Space people to get armed rockets ready for an assault? You could spend a year searching the moon for one tiny unknown alien camp…"

"Maybe not," snapped Durk tersely. "Out, Lloyd. I think I've got it. I'm going to try out this crate."

Lloyd scrambled back and slammed the hatchway shut. He watched wincingly as the saucer, without the slightest sound, rose fifty feet in the air. Then it shot forward wildly, straight for a nearby skyscraper. Miraculously, it spun and avoided a crash, then did several incredible flip-flops including a dive toward the ground that barely in time turned to an upward swoop.

Then, as if the pilot had gained a sure hand, the saucer shot up into the sky, achieving supersonic speed in one second. Lloyd gaped. He was on his way to the moon...

But a silvery speck reappeared and the saucer, glinting in the moonlight, spiraled down and landed neatly not twenty feet from Lloyd, who stood transfixed.

"Superb controls," sang Durk, stepping out. "Engineered so that even a baby or a moron can drive it easily and safely. It has all sorts of automatic anti-disaster gimmicks so that you can hardly crash if you tried." He took a breath and looked up at the crescent moon. "Before I go, I want to take something along." He scribbled on a scrap of paper and handed it to Lloyd. "Rustle that up right now, even if you have to use police to get it out of a closed chemical plant."

Lloyd did not question the command. Like the original Durk, this Durk double had a flashing mind that could leap to spectacular heights at times. What his idea was Lloyd could not guess. But whatever it was, it had some connection with the aliens and would lead to some sensational denouement.

Two hours later, a dozen big plastic drums had been loaded aboard the saucer.

"That's a big load," said Lloyd doubtfully.

Durk laughed scornfully. "That crate could carry ten times as much without feeling it. It has *power*, man. A magnitude more powerful than any propulsion system known to earth." He leaped in the hatchway finally, with the last wave at Lloyd.

"Good luck," breathed Lloyd, but he had little faith that he would see that face again, either singly or doubly.

* * * *

At the saucer's controls, Durk sat as if in a trance while he arrowed toward the moon. Nearing the lunar wastelands, his hand moved in zombie fashion as he manipulated the master control stick.

The saucer came down and hovered over a crater. Puzzled, Durk looked down. Then his head turned slightly and he drifted the ship over to the next crater. Automatically, its sensors adjusted to admit returning saucercraft, the crater's false bottom lifted like a lid. With a quiet smile of satisfaction, Durk guided his craft down into the sublunarian stronghold, knowing he had unerringly found the aliens.

From here on, Durk knew he would have to play it by ear. Still, the beehive atmosphere of the place did not surprise him. Carefully, he maneuvered his saucer to the side of the giant cavern, where others were parked. Landing gently, he peered cautiously out of the small bubble-top of the pilot's cupola.

The sight of the queer little men with their wraparound eyes and stiff-legged gait, as they appeared in the distance, did not startle him since he had seen them on earth at the raid on Recreate Labs. But when he spied three giant monster-men with a single eye like the Cyclops, he was taken aback. But into his mind leaped the explanation—*warriors!*

Uncanny. Yet Durk knew what it was. He was in rapport with the mind of his twin, Wright. And just as this thin telepathic thread between them had led him to the ABM hideout where Wright had been captive, so it had led him to the alien hideout here on the moon.

Not only that, but Durk had picked up more ESP impressions from Wright. It was all a confused, tangled mass of vagueness but here and there he had plucked out something clear-cut—such as the idea of warriors in an ant-like community. These telepathic tip-offs would help him, he hoped, in finding Wright and somehow rescuing him.

Sitting in his saucer inconspicuously and waiting, Durk sat up, seeing a human moving among the little men and huge warriors. A man, quite like an earthman. He fished *"drone"* out of the faint telepathic flow of his twin's subconscious mind.

And with it came an ill-defined but persistent impression that if he boldly emerged and walked out, he would not be molested. Durk frowned. Should he trust that telepathic "tip?" What if it were wrong, a distorted impression from Wright's mind that he had twisted around? Still, the impression grew stronger and Durk made up his mind to chance it.

He stepped from the hatchway unhurriedly, peered in all directions sharply. Nobody nearby at the moment. He began to stride away, following another "signal" in his mind telling him which way to go to find Wright.

It led him toward a tunnel leading away from the huge central "city." Just before he reached the arched entrance, several *workers*—that name too came to him—emerged, directly in his path.

Tensing, Durk gripped the holster of the laser-gun concealed in his astronaut jacket. But the little men merely gave a half-bow and twittered at him in the alien garble he had heard over radio before. It sounded like a deferential greeting, and they moved on without alarm.

In a flash, Durk added it up for himself. Roughly aware that this was a beehive society, from Wright's telepathic trailings, Durk saw that he had simply been taken for a humanlike drone. His astronaut jacket and uniform were sufficiently flamboyant, in three bright colors, to resemble the gaudy clothing of the drones. And the workers were of such low mental caliber that they lacked the sharpness to suspect anything wrong with this "drone."

Breathing in relief, Durk entered the tunnel. He stuck out his chest and strutted along, acting like he had seen the other drone act. But he faltered when he turned a corner and abruptly faced two huge warriors standing on guard. They eyed him suspiciously with their single eye. Could the warriors be fooled too?

Durk decided to brazen it out and walk between them. His heart sank when they growled in their native gabble at him, obviously asking questions about where he was going. Tossing his head autocratically and looking disdainful, Durk put up a silent finger as if dismissing them and their trivial talk. And kept on going.

It worked. Durk glanced back to see the warriors gripping weapons, but then relaxing and shrugging. They twittered to each other as if saying—"A snob, like all the drones."

Durk trembled now, in reaction to this dangerous moment. But with a bit more luck, he should finish his mission—which on the face of it was impossible. To boldly invade the enemy stronghold in one of their own craft... swagger through the halls like one of their drones... escape the suspicions of the workers and warriors... and snatch Wright from their hands—well, it was like dream stuff that could never happen.

Yet it was happening. Incredible, fantastic, unbelievable... but he was getting away with it. Fleetingly, Durk suspected most of his luck was due to the inferior qualities of the beehive society. On earth, no alien could pose as an earthman in a security-guarded place for a moment. Even the lowest-IQ guard would be suspicious and call the alarm. But a deep schism and lack of communication between the drone, worker, and warrior classes of the aliens worked in favor of Durk and his outrageous plan.

The unconscious ESP signal from Wright's brain was stronger now. A few more turns in the corridor and Durk stood before a door and knew that his twin was beyond it. But along with the ESP impressions he had followed there came, at times, twinges of pain. Mental pain. And now, outside the door, a stab of it was so intense that Durk almost felt it physically and had to bite his lips to keep from crying out.

Torture! Mental torture. That was what it must be. Wright was being subjected to some fiendish process of mental dissection. Another fierce stab of telepathic pain and Durk bunched all his muscles, in volcanic rage.

He waited only to gather in one more dim ESP image—that of three drones in white suits bending over Wright inside. Three aliens to account for...

CHAPTER 19

Durk kicked the door inward violently and sprang in a moment later, laser-gun already out and leveled. One brief glance showed him the three drones bending over the figure of Wright strapped down, with a humming ray-device clamped around his head.

The drones turned at the interruption. Durk's laser spat soundlessly and one drone went down with a surprised look, a neat hole burned through his skull, smoking a bit. The other two drones reacted as humans would when threatened and threw themselves aside.

One drone tried to dive behind apparatus but didn't quite make it. Durk's death-beam drilled through the middle of his body, puncturing vital organs. He died with one shrill scream.

But the third drone had reached a desk and yanked out a weapon. Swinging around he shot at Durk and a bolt of sizzling blue lightning scorched Durk's uniform at the left shoulder. The drone had no chance to try a second shot. A laser-hole got him in the leg, from a snap shot by Durk. Falling to one knee, the drone tried to raise his blast-gun. But Durk had had time to aim now and a smoking hole appeared exactly between his eyes. He fell over soundlessly.

Almost gagging at the vile smell of burning flesh, Durk recovered and darted to the table where Wright lay strapped. His face still twisted in previous pain, Wright's eyes fluttered open. They widened in disbelief.

"Durk," he croaked. "I'm dreaming…"

"No, you aren't," assured Durk. "It's really me and I'm going to get you out of this alien hellhole. Hold still now."

Durk was using his laser to burst the bonds holding Wright down. He sat up, pulling off the helmet he wore, hurling it against the wall furiously. "Mental probe… like a needle pinching every brain-cell… every shrieking nerve…" He held his head for a moment, moaning. Then, composing himself, he leaped off the table.

"Let's go, Durk."

Durk pulled him back from the door. "Not that way, two against the mob. Put on one of the drone's clothing and walk out in style."

Wright grinned, nodding. Before long he straightened up, wearing the many-colored costume of a drone. In the meantime, at the sudden thought, Durk had done the same. It was better than his astronaut costume for posing as a drone.

They walked out boldly, closing the door behind them. "No telling how soon they'll discover those bodies," whispered Wright, "and find out their prisoner is gone. How do we get out of the place?"

"In a flying saucer." Durk went on briefly to give the story.

"Clever," said Wright at the end, admiring his double and then flushing a bit. It was like patting himself on the back, for with the roles reversed, he would undoubtedly have done exactly the same. They tensed as they passed groups of workers, and once two warrior guards. But by simply marching haughtily past them without a word, they went unchallenged. It was not for the lowly workers or warriors to question the doings of the noble drones, nor take offense at their insulting attitudes.

"It's almost too easy," muttered Wright as they went on along the hallways.

Durk had something else on his mind. "You know, one thing utterly baffles me. If they knew there were two men aboard our spacecraft, why didn't they come after my life-rocket as soon as they captured you and saw only one man in the ship? Obviously, if one man escaped out of the two, he would bring the word of the Brain Blight immunity to earth."

"But they didn't know there were two men aboard," said Wright.

Durk stared at him blankly. "How could they miss, when they used a mind-sensor to monitor us?"

"But the monitor didn't show two minds." Wright was grinning strangely. "I figured it all out before. Their monitor only registered one mind because of that rapport we have between us—" Wright hesitated, not wanting to stress that and inflame Durk's suspicions again over their remarkable alikeness. "Well, to them it sounded like only one mind having a conversation with itself, just the way any man sometimes talks to himself."

Wright did not add that only two *identical* minds could so be accepted by a mind-sensor as being just a single mind. Only the unique situation of Wright-Durk and his recreated double being in the ship could have worked and nullified the mind-sensor. It had never revealed to the aliens that there were *two separate minds* and two men aboard the earth spacecraft.

And being too far away at the time to see the tiny life-rocket veer off, they had never suspected that a second man had escaped and that the man they captured was only half of a team.

Wright laughed wildly to himself. It was a cosmic joke on the aliens. With all their careful planning to prevent earth from getting the blight-immunity data, they had failed.

But then he sobered at something he had forgotten. He gripped Durk's arm.

"The anti-blight immunity—it's no good," he said hoarsely. "If we use it the aliens will simply shift to a new kind of Brain Bug able to override that immunity."

Durk had paled at those dread words.

"But why worry?" continued Wright. "We still have Recreate Labs and…" His voice ground to a halt and stark horror leaped into his eyes. "Wait… you told me of the raid on Recreate Labs, both by the ABM and the aliens. Was it destroyed?"

"Totally," nodded Durk.

"Then with the immunity cancelled out and Recreate Labs gone…" Wright half moaned. He did not have to finish the sentence. Instead he said, tonelessly, "The only sure thing would be to destroy this alien stronghold and end the menace forever. But earth's forces—mainly pioneering vehicles and freightage haulers—are too weak to mount any kind of military attack on this place. The aliens can battle them off easily and continue their damnable campaign of wiping out earth's brainpower." He clenched his fists. "If only this alien nest could be wiped out, all our problems would be solved. But that's impossible."

"Is it?" asked Durk quietly. Wright glanced at him sharply, but Durk pursed his lips and said no more.

They had now reached the main portion of the beehive city, the vast, cellular cavern in which rested the flying saucer landing field. Cautiously, they walked toward it. Durk wound among the parked saucers and led the way to the one he had come in. He recognized it because it was parked between two other craft of different design.

"Aboard," he said calmly, "is the means to destroy all the aliens, every one."

Wright could only stare in disbelief.

Leading the way aboard, Durk pointed to the dozen big drums stacked in the cabin. "Notice they're not steel drums but wax-coated plastics. They hold pure yellow phosphorus. You know what that stuff does when it's exposed to air or oxygen."

"It begins to smoke and soon ignites spontaneously," returned Wright, sudden excitement in his voice. "It then burns fiercely and produces enormous volumes of phosphoric oxides, all of them extremely poisonous. Great, Durk. But what gave you the idea?"

"Again a faint telepathic impression from your mind—not a message but just a vague glimmer—that the alien place was a *beehive*. And to get rid of a bee nest or hive, you smoke them out. Or smother them. Help me roll the barrels out before anyone gets suspicious."

In the moon's light gravity, it did not take long to roll the drums out beside the saucer. Durk drew his laser-gun, waving Wright back. He neatly sliced one barrel in half. The two halves of yellow waxy substance that were exposed instantly began to smoke as the intensely active phosphorus combined with oxygen in the air. The edges began to melt slowly and ran. The fumes became thicker.

Both men coughed, holding their hands at their mouths. "As soon as I open all the barrels, we go," said Durk grimly, using his laser on the next barrel.

But at that moment a shout was heard. Swinging around, Wright paled. Several alien drones were running toward them and yelling, followed by a band of giant warriors.

"They've caught onto us," said Wright hoarsely. "They'll get here before you have time to slice open all the drums…"

"But they must all be opened to make sure this entire place is *fumigated*, to rid it of those alien vermin," snarled Durk, face savage. "I'll stay and finish the job. You go, Wright. The saucer has an automatic pilot that takes the shop out of the crater. Press the big red button. Once out in space, you'll have time to figure out the controls and fly to earth. Get *going!*"

"But you'll never get out alive," said Wright frantically.

"Who cares?"

"Ellen cares," exploded Wright. "And Randy and Wendy. You *must* return to them, Durk."

"Why me?" shot back Durk, slicing another barrel. "Why not the *real thing?*"

Wright jerked. "You know?"

"Of course," said Durk the double. "I suspected it for some time. It was all clinched when I heard of Recreate Labs during the raid by the ABM and the saucer attack. Everything fell into place—that I was your recreate."

He glanced anxiously at the running figures, now coming across the landing field and getting close.

"Listen. I'll have to talk fast. I can't go back to Ellen, knowing I'm a fraud, a copy, a gingerbread man baked in a lab. Go back, Wayne Durk. After all, you've only been away from Ellen a year and a half and lived with her for many years before—and will for many years to come. Me, I've *only* taken your place for that year and a half. The rest is sham, mockery, a shadow life." He used one hand to shove Wright toward the saucer. "Go, you fool. Yes, you have a year's 'amnesia'—the year you were lost in space—but you can work it out somehow and cover it up."

His eyes became fierce. "And swear, Wayne Durk... swear that you'll never tell Ellen about me, your recreate. *Swear it.*"

"But I'm not going," snapped Durk-Wright, inflexibly. "If one of us has to die, let it be both of us." He grinned mirthlessly. "It'll really be only *one* man dying anyway."

That's as far as he got before the laser-gun, swung by Durk, thudded down on his head. Sobbing in haste, the Durk double scooped up the limp body and flung it into the saucercraft. Then he punched the red button and leaped out.

An auto-mechanism slammed shut the door and the robot pilot took the saucer up in a soaring glide.

Swiftly the Durk recreate turned to slice the remaining barrels of phosphorus. Then he turned smiling to face the oncoming mob of vengeful bee-men. His laser cut down a dozen before a warrior's saw-toothed club slashed at him.

But even as the Durk double went down, fatally wounded, the clouds of poisonous phosphorus vapors swept over the group and downed them all. They twitched and writhed briefly, then lay still.

And the cloud of phosphorus death went on, seeking out every nook and cranny of the underground hideaway. The aliens had no gasmasks, no means of quenching the lethal fire as the phosphorus melted from its own heat of combustion and spread out into a wide burning pool, consuming all in its way and choking the air with fumes. Nor could the beehive people escape. Beyond the double airlock system of the crater-lid lay the dead, airless moon.

The hum of the giant beehive slowly died down as the last figures staggered around in the white mists of death. A great bloated figure filled with eggs also choked her last...

* * * *

Wayne Durk—again the one and only Wayne Durk—came to in space, seeing the moon below him. Faintly, he could see a dark crater's floor with white wisps of vapor escaping around the cracks of a circular lid.

A million bee-aliens had died—and one man.

Silently, Durk raised a hand and saluted.

On earth later, at night, a flying saucer streaked down silently from the sky, miraculously came to an instant halt, then slowly settled down with a falling-leaf motion.

Durk stepped out. For a long moment he stared up at the silvery crescent of the moon, filled with an infinite sadness. But perhaps it was more merciful than not that his recreate had met oblivion—and peace. There would have been no peace for him back on earth. Nor little for all the other recreates still in existence.

But Recreate Labs were gone. There was no further need for them. A necessary evil, they had served their purpose for a time. Or had they? Had enough mindpower been added to the world brainbank to brace the foundations of civilization, already cracking? Could a badly crippled society hold out until the next generation, by blessed genetic laws, brought forth a new crop of high genius, which was totally missing on earth now?

The cold, silent stars gave no answer.

Durk shivered and turned, a strange thought swirling into his mind. He had paradoxically died to save the world—and yet he lived…

But now he was no longer a double man. Whimsically came the thought that neither was he a "single" man. With an uplift of spirit and a weary smile, Durk walked toward the door where Ellen would be waiting.